Utterly
Me,
Clarice
Bean

Friday

This is me, Clarice Bean.

I am not an only child, but I sometimes
wish I was.

My family is six people, which is sometimes
too many.

Not always, just sometimes.

Mainly my dad is mostly in an office answering
the phone and going, "I can't talk now, I'm
up to my ears in it."

Mum is always gribbling about pants on the floor and shoes on the sofa.

She says, "This house doesn't clean itself you know.

Who do you think does everything around here?

Mr Nobody?

I don't get paid to pick up your smelly socks! If I did I'd be a rich woman." etc etc non-non-stop.

I am the third oldest and I think it would have been a good idea if I was the youngest too.

I am not quite sure why my mum and dad wanted to have more children after me.

They don't need another one and it's a shame because he is spoiling it for everyone else.

He is called Minal Cricket and he tends to be utterly a nuisance.

He is non-stop whining and causing other people to get themselves in trouble.

You might think
it would be a
relief to come to school,
but if you do,
then obviously you don't know
some of the people in my class.
Naming no names,
i.e. Grace Grapello,
what a show-off.

Sometimes I stare boredly into space,
thinking utterly of
nothing.

This makes Mrs Wilberton very irritated.

I get on her nerves.

I know this because she is always telling me I do.

To be honest, Mrs Wilberton is not my favourite person on the planet of Earth.

Unfortunately, I am from Earth and she is my teacher.

Mrs Wilberton says I have got utterly not a speck of concentration.

I am trying to prove her wrong about this by trying to remember to concentrate.

I think about it all the time. I am so desperately trying not to not concentrate and I say to myself, 'Don't drift off like you did yesterday.'

And then I start thinking about how I drifted off yesterday and how I was thinking I must listen to Mrs Wilberton and all the things she is telling me.

And then I am wondering,
how does all this stuff she is telling me
fit into my head?

And then I am wondering if I should have a clear out
of the stuff I don't need anymore –
you know,
like when my dad cleared out the attic,
except we all decided
we needed
everything
and he just had to put it all back again.

But maybe valuable space is being taken up in
my
head
with not the important things and

that

is why

I can't

c o n c e n t r a t e

because all my concentration space

has been used up

on things like,

'Elbows off the table',

and,

'Don't pinch your brother', and

pointless

not needed

things

which

don't matter.

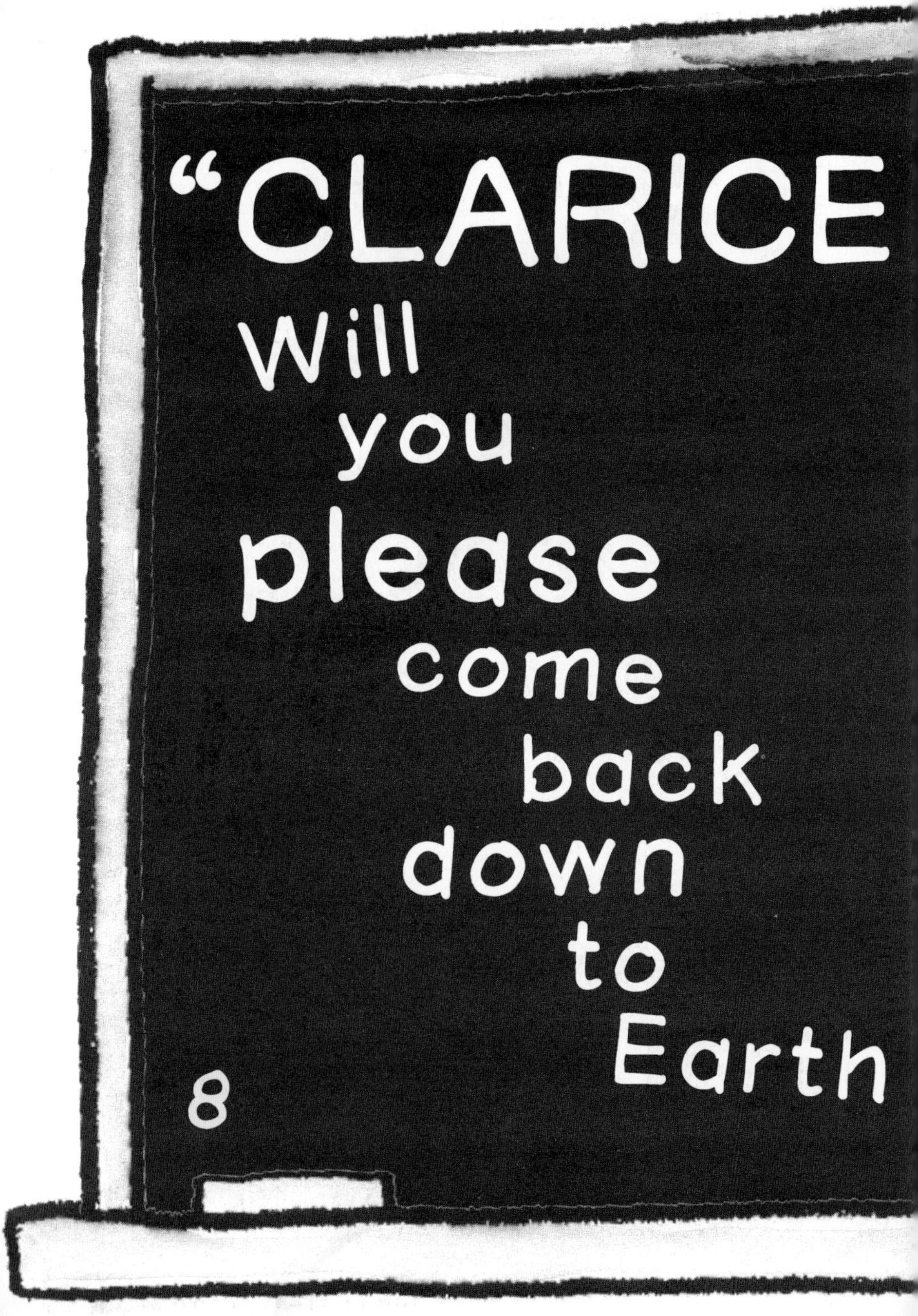
"CLARICE
Will
you
please
come
back
down
to
Earth

BEAN!

this instant!"

It's Mrs Wilberton.

You
can
tell
by
her
honking
goose
voice.

She says,

"Clarice Bean,
you are utterly lacking in the
concentration department.
A common housefly has got
more ability to apply itself!"

And I want to say,

"You are utterly lacking in the
manners department, Mrs Wilberton,
and a rhinoceros has got more
politeness than you."

But I don't say it because Mrs Wilberton is allowed to say rude things about me and I am not allowed to say them back.

That is the rules of school.

Then Mrs Wilberton says, "Right class, I am announcing the very exciting subject of this year's school open day competition."

Mrs Wilberton doesn't look one bit excited but I think it would take an elephant running into the classroom waving its arms about to get Mrs Wilberton hopping around.

Anyway, everybody must pair up and think of an exhibit that they would like to put together and have on show for when all the parents traipse in to see just what their little darlings have been getting up to.

Of course, me and Betty Moody are a pair because we are utterly best friends.

Mrs Wilberton says the project must be based on a book we have read and learnt something from.

It sounds **utterly** dreary to me.

When I get home I go straight upstairs to the airing cupboard.

I take a mini cheese with me because they are my favourite things at the moment, and you never know when you might want something to nibble.

The airing cupboard is a good place to be on your own by yourself.

And it's where I like to read my book.

You need a torch and it is lucky that I got one for Christmas.

I had to ask for it and put a note up the chimney for Father Christmas.

I don't think I believe in Father Christmas but Mum and Dad want me to, so I write to him anyway.

I wrote, 'Dear Father Christmas, If you are true, please can I have a torch, and if you are not true, then please can someone else get me one?'

I think it is important to keep your options open,

because you never know what is the actual in fact truth these days.

Granny says the world is a very mysterious place, what with men in space and so on.

She says, "After all, who would have thought you would one day be able to send someone a picture down the telephone, or cook a leg of lamb in five minutes?"

I didn't used to be so much of a reader, it just happened when Granny gave me a book called THERE WAS A GIRL CALLED RUBY and Mum says there and then I turned into a bookworm.

THERE WAS A GIRL CALLED RUBY is from a whole series of books called THE RUBY REDFORT COLLECTION.

Betty Moody and me utterly love them.

They are about this amazing girl – she's a bit like a detective but she's only eleven.

She doesn't have any brothers and sisters and gets
to go on these sort of adventures.

The
most
I
do
is
go
to
the
local
shop
on
my
own.

Ruby Redfort lives in this mad sort of house and her parents are fabulously rich and she has an actual butler man who gets to do all these things for her.

He's called Hitch, which is his last name.

You only get to call butlers by their last name – it's normal in the world of butlers.

Ruby Redfort drives to school in a helicopter sometimes, and has these gadgets and things.

Even Ruby Redfort's PE kit isn't normal.

Her trainers have special springing power so she can jump over her enemies, and her swimming costume has a built-in propeller so she can swim as fast as a mackerel.

Ruby gets post in the mail all of her own – imagine that!

It's all interesting and top secret from other detectives and government prime ministers and people, and it is full of clues in strange codes.

But no one ever suspects anything, because why would they?

That's the most ingenious thing about Ruby
Redfort – she doesn't need a disguise because
who would expect a schoolgirl to be a master
investigator agent?
No one, that's who!

I only get post at birthdays, so I've started
sending off for things.
There's lots of free things you can get them to
send you if you fill out the coupon.
Mum calls it junk mail but I think it's interesting
to get post, even if it is about thermal vests.
My dad gets post with
PRIVATE
written on it,
so for all I know he is a secret agent himself.
I have had a sneak at one of the letters and there
were lots of numbers and dates and then some
words in red saying
FINAL REMINDER.
It's all utterly suspicious.

And the other day, Dad said that,
'There might be a reshuffle going on at work',
and that he
'will have to jump through hoops',
if he wants to get
'a share of the pie'.
He says, "The big cheese has been making noises
and some people might be left out in the cold if

they don't keep their
eye on the ball.
But that's the
way the cookie
crumbles."
I'm not sure what he
was talking about.
Betty Moody says it
is probably almost
definitely code.

Dad says, "I can assure you if I was a secret agent I would go and be secret somewhere hot and sunny with a nice beach and no telephones."

Dad usually has to have a telephone with him at all times. He utterly mustn't be uncontactable for even a second.

It would be very hard for me to be a secret agent because my whole family are always poking their noses into my private affairs and to do anything secretly is extremely impossible.

Betty says you need to have a good cover story and gadgets, which are disguised as other everyday objects.

Like i.e. for example, Ruby Redfort's toaster also converts into a special fax machine.

And if you press the button
d
o
w
n,
a secret message gets transmitted from Ruby's boss
at HQ and

is written onto the toast.

And then after Ruby Redfort has read it, she can just eat the evidence so no one will ever see it. Betty also says, "You must be confident as a cucumber in order not to arouse suspicion." Ruby's parents know utterly nothing about her secret life as a mystery solver and special agent because Ruby gives them nothing to be suspicious about.

Sometimes Ruby barely gets back from Russia or somewhere before her parents come in to kiss her goodnight.

Sometimes she does this trick of stuffing pillows under the duvet so it looks like she's actually asleep when really she's fifteen-and-a-bit thousand miles away and not wearing her pyjamas at all but probably instead a furry jacket, up a steep mountain.

I tell Betty, "I tried doing the pillows down the bed and it doesn't work, not if your mum is like mine and checks to see if you have brushed your teeth."

I say, "I don't think even Ruby Redfort could trick my mum."

Betty says, "What Ruby Redfort would do is to simply spray the smell of toothpaste in her room so her mother would smell the minty freshness and would just think she must have brushed her teeth and so wouldn't bother to check."

Of course, it's so simple!

When you think about it.

The other equipment you simply must have if you are going to be a secretive agent is a telephone.

Ruby Redfort has telephones all over the place – even in the bathroom.

Sometimes Hitch the butler carries them about on a tray.

Betty Moody's got one in her room.

I asked Dad if I could get a telephone in my room.

He laughed in a funny way for about almost 9 minutes.

That's the thing about Betty's parents, they are really nice.

Mr and Mrs Moody always say, "Call me Cecil," and, "Call me Mol," and even Betty calls them Cecil and Mol.

They let Betty get up to whatever she wants really, and she goes to bed whenever she likes.

Betty Moody is an only child.

Well, an almost only child. She has a brother called Zack who is over twenty years old.

He lives in a flat and has a girlfriend who is from Japan.

I have an oldish brother called Kurt.

Not many people get to see Kurt because he is usually in his room being alone. His room is full of gloom and a strange unpleasant smell.

He keeps everything on the floor and no tidying is ever allowed.

Mum says, "It is all part of being a teenager and he will grow out of it one day."

I say, "When?"

Dad says, "Don't hold your breath."

Which means it could take a while.

Monday

The Ruby book I am reading right now at this exact instant is called RUBY REDFORT RULES.

All the books start off the same way:

On a street called Cedarwood Drive was an ultra-modern house, white and gleaming with glass. And in that house lived a most unusual little girl, daughter to Brant and Sabina Redfort, socialites.

Brant and Sabina called their little girl Ruby, but to those in the know she was Ruby Redfort — secret agent, undercover detective and mystery solver.

There is a picture of her house and a map of the secret getaway tunnels.

The books always start off really calm and cosy so you just don't know what you are in for.

It was a wonderful morning. Mrs Digby drew back the curtains and the sun splashed on Ruby Redfort's angelic face.

"Muffins or French toast?" enquired the ever-thoughtful housekeeper.

"Muffins," yawned Ruby, stuffing her feet into remarkably fluffy slippers.

"Rightio, Miss Ruby. I'll just go run you a bath...take your time, no need to rush yourself."

You see, you can't help thinking it's going to be utterly boring. But just you wait.

Ruby could tell it was going to be a fabulous day. She just had a good feeling about...

"Mum says

　　you better get out of bed
　　　　right now,
and if you want milk on your Sugar Puffs,
　　　　too bad,
　　　there isn't any."

That's my sister Marcie – you can tell by
the rudeness.

Mum says when manners were being handed out
Marcie must have been in the toilet.

I have to
　　hop
　　　downstairs

because I only have one slipper. Our dog,
Cement, buried the other one in the garden and
we can't find it.

It will probably be discovered in a hundred years
from now by archaeological diggers who will say
it is fascinating and give it to a museum.

When I get downstairs, the whole
kitchen is full of a bad mood.
Marcie won't talk to Mum, and
Kurt won't talk to Marcie.
Grandad isn't talking to anyone
because he hasn't plugged himself
into his hearing-aid.
Minal is talking to me
but I wish he wouldn't.
Minal is a niggling gnat
and I have to have him sleeping in my room.
Sometimes, when I want to keep him out,
I pile lots of gubbins against the door.
He is five.
Who wants to share a room with
a five-year-old brother? I don't
even need a five-year-old brother.
I already have one who is a
teenager called Kurt and
that is enough brothers
for anyone.

Minal is going, "What time did the spider go
to the dentist?"

I don't bother to listen to the answer because
it won't be funny.

I am trying to read the back of the cereal
packet because there is a good offer on rubber
pencil-tops.

Minal is going, "Spider clock!

D'ya get it? D'ya get it? Spider clock!"

I say, "No."

He is joggling me, which makes me spill my
orange juice down my jumper.

So I give him a Chinese burn.

Mum says, "Clarice, you are really
behaving like an earwig!

Can you get your coat on
and zip off to school quick smart,
no funny business. And pull
your socks up, don't forget
your packed lunch, and by the way,
you've dribbled down your front."

Sometimes, if I can, I read my book walking to school.

Ruby took the elevator down from the kitchen to the front door.

"See you, Hitch," she called to the butler as she stepped inside the sleek black limo which was waiting outside. Ruby flicked on the onboard TV, she liked to tune into her favourite cartoons before the school day began. She enjoyed the ride; it was so hassle free...

"Clarice Beean, **Clarice Beean!** **Wait for me.** I'm right **behind you!**"

It's the boy from over the wall, Robert Granger. I try to ignore him and carry on reading my book.

"On second thoughts," said Ruby to her chauffeur, "I'll walk."

After all, it was a fabulous day and this way she could stop in at the mini-market and pick up some of that bubble-gum she liked.

"Clarice Beean, I know you can hear me!"

Robert Granger!

He drives me just about loopy.

Sometimes he just sits on the wall waiting for me to pop my head out of the door.

I spend half my time trying to get rid of him.

Mum says I am lucky and that I should take it as a compliment.

She says not everyone has someone who wants to be with them so much that they follow them around all day.

I say she is welcome to him, she can have him skipping behind her in his anorak – see how lucky she feels.

Ruby Redfort has an annoying neighbour too, but he's 70ish and so isn't in her school class or anything but he is always poking his nose into other people's businesses, so in that way he is very similar to Robert Granger.

Mr Parker stuck his nose out of his front door and sniffed very loudly.

"Is that that Redfort child? I've told you before, keep off my grass! Do your parents know where you are? Shouldn't you be at school? I've got a good mind to call them myself."

Ruby Redfort just acted like she couldn't hear a thing.

"Good morning, Mr Parker," called Ruby cheerily. "How are you today?"

This always made Mr Parker madder than ever.

I rush into school and Betty Moody is there
already and she is wearing some strange fancy
shoes that are foreign.
Betty Moody travels the world with her mum

and dad and they have
friends all over the planet,
even in China which is
a gersquillion kilometres
and miles from
here at the
very least.
Betty's
parents
say it is
essential
for a child to
see the world
if they are
to become
a well-rounded
individual.

They say travelling the world is the best
education a child could have,
and they often fly Betty off somewhere
at utterly just a moment's notice.
It's most unusual.
I wish Robert Granger would go off around
the world.
He comes marching up to me and Betty and
says, "Have you thought of your book exhibit
idea yet because you should because there is
going to be a mystery prize for the best book
exhibit and you will get your name written on
a little silver cup which goes in the glass trophy
cupboard and everyone will see it, it says so on
the board and me and Arnie Singh have thought
of a really good exhibit and we are going to
win."
Which of course is utterly unlikely, knowing
them.
It turns out Robert Granger and Arnie Singh are
doing an exhibit of dinosaurs.

They say they have got an original dinosaur's prehistoric bones, but I know they are chicken bones from Robert's Sunday lunch.

I say, "Those bones are too small to be dinosaur bones."

And they say, "They are from a very tiny dinosaur."

I say, "There weren't any tiny dinosaurs, that is a chicken."

They say, "It is a chicken dinosaur."

I say, "That's interesting. I didn't know you could buy dinosaurs in the supermarket."

Mind you,
it's got our minds whirring.
We look at the tiny winners' cup in the glass trophy cupboard.
We really want to win it, and of course our heads are blank with no ideas.
Also, we are wondering what the mystery prize could be.

Winner

I think it might be a walkie-talkie and Betty thinks it will be one of those cameras which gives you the pictures straight away.
Whatever it is, we want it.

After school, I go back to Betty Moody's house, so we can talk about our exhibit.
I love going round to the Moodys', it's really fun, and sometimes supper is just twiglets and a fizzy drink!
Usually though, Mr Moody-Call-Me-Cecil says, "Let's go out to the *Wah Chung.*"
Which is a Chinese restaurant, it's very smart with chairs of purpley velvet.

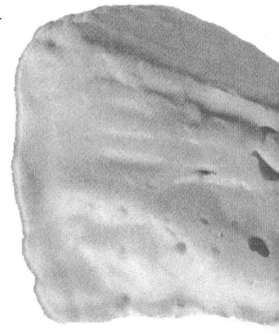

Other times he makes dinner out of whatever
is in the cupboard – maybe just a potato and
a strange-smelling cheese.

The Moodys live in a house that's modern, just
like Ruby Redfort does.

You have to go upstairs to the kitchen.

It's

amazing.

When you go in it's straight away 'shoes off and special slippers on'.

They learnt that in Japan.

I have told Mum about it.

She says, "Clarice Bean! The times I have asked you to please take your shoes off and will you? No!"

It's true,

but it's funny because at the Moodys' house it feels like fun.

We end up hardly talking about the book competition at all because we can't stop talking about Ruby Redfort.

Me and Betty are crazily reading the whole series.

We can't stop. And when we have finished we read them over again.

I have just got to this bit where Ruby Redfort is standing for Class President

and they are having a school election

to vote for who is best.

Naturally, Mrs Drisco, Ruby's teacher, is not pleased about this because Ruby and Mrs Drisco do not see eye to eye. And of course Ruby has lots of good ideas for changing things, like e.g. making breaks longer.

I just wish there were more Ruby books. I am thinking of writing to Patricia F Maplin Stacey who is the author and telling her that she should write a bit more quickly.

Mrs Moody-Call-Me-Mol says, "Why don't you? People always love to hear how much other people enjoy their books."

Betty's mum knows about this because she is in fact a writer.

She is going off to sign books abroad in another country on Wednesday.

She is utterly well-known and you can buy her books in all the good bookshops.

So

we

write:

Dear Patricia F Maplin Stacey,

We are avidish readers of the Ruby Redfort series
and we have read all of them at least once.
What we would like to know is when is the next Ruby
Redfort book coming out and what will it be called?

Also, on page a hundred and 6, chapter eight of
Run for it Ruby

Why did the arch villain Hogtrotter not double-check that he had locked the cellar door?

And also, on page 33 you said Ruby was wearing her glasses and then later on you say she couldn't see well because she didn't have her reading glasses.

Eagerly awaiting your reply.

Betty P Moody and Clarice Bean Tuesday.

p.s. We think you should write a bit faster.

We write two letters, one from each of us, in case one gets lost in the post. Mol gives us stamps so we can post them tomorrow.

She asks us what we are up to at school and we tell her about the boring book competition which we want to win.

And she says, "Why do you have to pick a boring book?"

And she's right, why do we?

Except that we can't find one which is interesting which is also about learning.

Tuesday

The next day I am a bit anxious because me and Betty Moody still haven't thought of a book project.

Also, I am late because I can't stop myself reading RUBY REDFORT RULES.

Ruby sauntered into school, not bothering to hurry. After all, she was already 20 minutes late, what difference would another 5 make? She could always come up with an excuse. She had to get past Mrs Bexenheath, the school secretary, but that wasn't hard.

Mrs Bexenheath was no match for Ruby's excuses. No matter how hard the poor secretary tried, she just couldn't get Ruby to admit she was up to something.

It was Mrs Drisco who was the problem. No one was so strict as Mrs Drisco. Mrs Drisco made the evil Count von Viscount seem like a pussycat.

Ruby swaggered into the classroom and slumped down at her desk, lolling back in her chair. But to Ruby Redfort's enormous surprise, a telling-off did not follow, and instead Mrs Drisco beamed a friendly smile at her.

Mrs Drisco was being nice! Now that didn't seem right.

And as the lesson wore on, Ruby realized

that she wasn't bored! It was unthinkable to find Mrs Drisco's lessons anything but boring.

Something was definitely a bit fishy.

Had Mrs Drisco been turned into some kind of a Martian? Or had she been replaced by an impostor Mrs Drisco?

Too bad Mrs Wilberton hasn't been turned into a Martian. First of all, she gives me a mean look for lateness, and then she says, "I hope everybody has had a good think about what their book project will be. Anyone who hasn't chosen a book will be given one by me."

These words give me the shivers

because I know the kind of book Mrs Wilberton would pick.

Probably something like the secret life of a snail, or ballet, or snails that do ballet.

Betty and me look at each other and I make a face which means, 'help what shall we do?'

And she makes a face which means, 'how should I know?'

I am beginning to panic because if we can't think of anything then we will be in trouble and we will get a telling-off and then we will have to do one of Mrs Wilberton's dreary ideas.

Why hasn't Betty Moody come up with a good plan?

She is good at thinking of things which will keep Mrs Wilberton happy.

She utterly never gets in trouble.

It's true!

Never!

It's as if Betty has been zapped by the dastardly Count von Viscount.

It's like that bit in WHO WILL RESCUE RUBY REDFORT? when Count von Viscount tries to brainwash Ruby and steal all her good ideas.

He does it by making his eyes go goggly and before you know it you are under his spell.

Mrs Wilberton is going round the class – she is almost at me.

Alexandra Holker says she is doing her exhibit on the olden day times because she loves the past.

She says she is going to dress up in an ancient outfit and pretend she is from a hundred years ago and give out Victorian fudges. She got the idea from a book called *The Victorians*.

I have to admit, I wish I had thought of that.

And my cousin Noah and my friend Suzie Woo say they are doing their project on a book called *Global Grub* which is food from around the world, and they are going to have actual real life cookery in their exhibit.

Mrs Wilberton is almost about to say my name

and I can feel my stomach niggling with nerves, but just as she says, "Clarice Bean, what is your book competition entry?" Mrs Marse pops her head around the door and says, "Mrs Wilberton, Mr Pickering would like a word."

And then, just like that,

she beetles off.

After the break, Mrs Wilberton is huffing and puffing about something or other.

It's probably Karl Wrenbury's fault.

It usually is.

Karl Wrenbury is the naughtiest boy in my school and he is in my class.

He gets in trouble at least once a day.

One time he got into the caretaker's cupboard and stole some signs which said

THIS TOILET IS OUT OF ORDER!

He stuck them on all the doors, including Mr Pickering's office.

He got sent home for that.

Mrs Marse says he is probably hyperactive and that he should be kept off the sugary drinks. Mrs Wilberton says there is no excuse for bad behaviour and that Karl Wrenbury is just determined to be a disruptive influence and spoil it for the others.

I overheard her talking to Mr Skippard, the caretaker. She said, "I blame the parents."

And Mr Skippard said, "I couldn't agree more."

Mrs Wilberton says, "I am disappointed to tell you that somebody, naming no names, you know who you are, has been messing about before school and has flooded the boys' toilets."

I am a bit fidgety in case it is me, although
I haven't even been in the boys' toilets, ever.
It turns out it is Karl Wrenbury and also
Toby Hawkling.

They have to go and see Mr Pickering and they
don't come back.

When it's time to go home, I go to my peg to
put my coat on, but something funny has
happened to the sleeves and it has a zip instead of
buttons. The exactly same thing has happened to
the other coats.

It turns out all the coats have managed to get on
the wrong pegs. It takes ages to find mine.

I wonder how it happened – Karl Wrenbury
wasn't even at school this afternoon.

Spooky.

On the way back to my house I have to stop off
to buy some essentials, which is mainly a packet
of crisps. Unfortunately when I come out of the
shop, Robert Granger is standing outside.

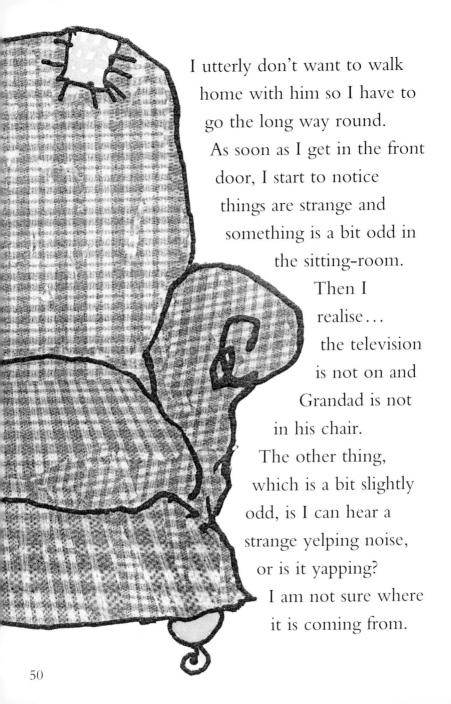

I utterly don't want to walk
home with him so I have to
go the long way round.
As soon as I get in the front
door, I start to notice
things are strange and
something is a bit odd in
the sitting-room.
Then I
realise...
the television
is not on and
Grandad is not
in his chair.
The other thing,
which is a bit slightly
odd, is I can hear a
strange yelping noise,
or is it yapping?
I am not sure where
it is coming from.

It's not from Cement anyway, because he is standing next to me, eating the message pad.

I try and wrestle it from him because I can see that he is about to swallow a message from someone but I don't know who.

The only words I can read say, 'didn't have time to tell you, but going to Rus...'

What can it mean?

Who didn't have time to tell who? And why are they in a rush?

I am just wondering what to do when the telephone rings.

It's Mum. She says, "Clarice, could you tell your brother to put the dinner in the oven."

I say, "There's something fishy happening. I can hear someone yapping..."

She says, "Mrs Pargett...not like that! You'll do yourself a mischief...I'm coming! Don't move! Wait there!"

And then the line goes dead.

Mum works at the old people's centre and is teaching them dancing.

She says dancing can be very dangerous if your
hips aren't what they once were.
Anyway I get my little notebook out
and I write down:
Very strange occurrence in the sitting-room.
That's the kind of thing Ruby Redfort would say.

Missing Grandad
and a yelping or is it a yapping noise?

Mum doesn't seem bothered.
What is going on?

I underline that several times
because
that is the
big
question.
Kurt shrivels the supper,
and it tastes of burnt but that isn't odd.
What's spooking me is that he seems happy!
I will tell Betty Moody about it tomorrow.

Wednesday

As soon as I get up, I start reading again. I even read walking downstairs to breakfast.

> Ruby Redfort sauntered into the kitchen where the wonderful Mrs Digby was already preparing pancakes.
> They smelt unbelievably mouth-watering...

Dad says, "What would you like for breakfast?"
I say, "Pancakes."
Dad says, "If you want pancakes, you can make them yourself."
I say, "Alright, I will then."
Mum says, "We've run out of eggs."

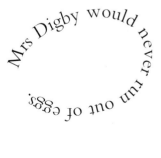

Mrs Digby would never run out of eggs.

When I get to school, Betty Moody is nowhere
to be seen.

I wonder what has happened. She is utterly,
absolutely never not ever late for class.

Except very rarely.

Maybe she has got the chickenpox or an
infectious temperature.

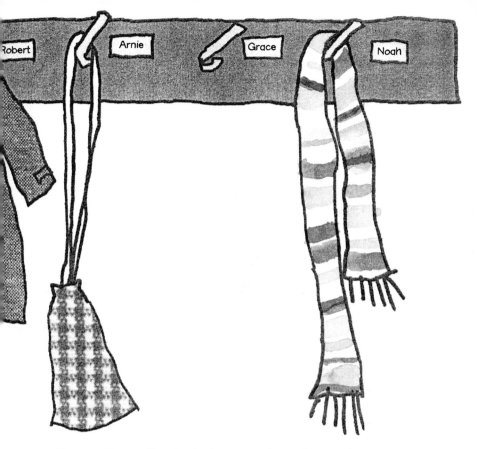

Grace Grapello isn't here either, hoorah!
The worst thing is there is no escaping telling
Mrs Wilberton what our project is going to be.
I am thinking, 'What would Ruby Redfort do
in this situation?'
Ruby Redfort can always think of a snappy
answer when Mrs Drisco is on her tail.

She would say something like:

"Well, Mrs Drisco, the thing is, I was walking along, minding my own business when, what do you know, but I got pounced on by this whole group of wild cats and, in my desperate attempt to fight them off, I hit my head and am now suffering from amnesia."

Which is forgetting your memory.

"And so you see, Mrs Drisco, I am unable to tell you what my book exhibit is, on account of the fact that it has been wiped from my mind, and if you don't believe me, just call our butler, Hitch."

And then Mrs Drisco might say, "Well, Miss Redfort, I think I might just do that."

And of course, when she calls Hitch he says,

"Oh yes, Mrs Drisco, I am afraid that's exactly what happened."

Hitch always backs Ruby up.

I wish I had a butler, but Dad says butlers are very expensive.

"Clarice Bean! For the third and final time,

would you please answer my question!"
And before I can stop myself I say, "Umm
wha...what was the question, Mrs Drisco?"
Mrs Wilberton looks at me with scrunkled eyes
and says, "Well, missy, it may be too much for
you to remember, but everyone else here knows
that my name is Mrs

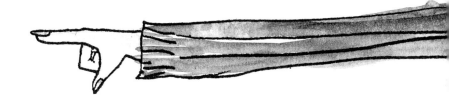

W.I.L.B.E.R.T.O.N.

That's Wilberton."

Mrs Wilberton says, "The question was, what is
your book exhibit going to be about and are you
going to enter the competition?"
I am looking down at my desk, staring at my
book RUBY REDFORT RULES and I am just about

to tell Mrs Wilberton the amnesia excuse when something accidentally pops out of my mouth.

I don't really mean to say it but it's a bit like Ruby Redfort often says, "Sometimes the answer is right under your nose. And sometimes you just have to come up with an answer even if it is maybe sort of the wrong answer."

What I say is, "Yes, Mrs Wilberton, me and Betty Moody will be doing an exhibit on Ruby Redfort – secret agent and arch detective."

Everyone is in a stunned silence because they wish they'd thought of it.

Mrs Wilberton is in a stunned silence because she doesn't think it is such a good idea.

I know this because she makes her mouth go all tight and then says, "I do not think this is such a good idea."

She says, "Just what do you imagine you have learnt from these books?"

And of course, that's the catch, I can't think of anything I have learnt from them but I am sure

Betty will think of something.
I walk home in a utterly

excited mood.

Ruby Redfort was thrilled! She had got the better of that Mrs Drisco. Well, this time anyway.

Mrs Drisco was determined to thwart Ruby's attempts to be Class President and stop her from making the changes to school uniform and lunch breaks that everybody was crying out for.

When I get home, I go to telephone Betty to tell her the good news but no one is picking up the receiver.
I am beginning to get worried.
Maybe all the Moodys are ill in bed with the chickenpox.
But even if they were, they would still be able to answer the telephone because they have

telephones in their bedrooms in case of emergencies like the chickenpox.

I can hear that yapping again, and it's coming from Grandad's room, and there is no doubt that it is not Cement because Cement does not yap. Also, Grandad is out giving him his walk, he has left a note.

I look through the keyhole and I think I can see something moving and it can't be our cat, Fuzzy, because he is standing next to me. Something is peculiar.

I decide to have a quick peek in his room, but just then I hear Grandad opening the front door, and so I quickly pick up the telephone and pretend to be talking to Mrs Stampney, our neighbour.

This is exactly the kind of thing that Ruby Redfort would do.

The only problem is, Grandad hears me pretending to be chatting to Mrs Stampney who,

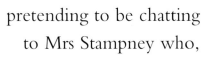

P.S. I do not like one iota, and then Grandad asks me to ask Mrs Stampney if he can borrow her spare dog basket for some strange reason. Now that means I will have to specially ring Mrs Stampney, otherwise he will smell a rat.

That never happens to Ruby Redfort.
Then Grandad says, "By the way, your friend Betty called this morning."
I eagerly say, "Did she leave a message?"
And he says, "She said something about rushing, I didn't hear what else she was talking about because the line was crackly."
Rushing? Why was Betty Moody rushing?

Was something chasing her?

After supper, I am keen to get back to my book.
I can't sit and read in the airing cupboard
because, mysteriously, my torch has gone missing
and may well be stolen.

Instead I have to read in my room.

At the moment I am reading this bit – it's very
exciting – I am literally on the edge of my wits.

> Night fell like a cloak over the city. There
> wasn't a single star twinkling. It was as if there
> was no sky at all.

You see, already it's gripping.

> Ruby Redfort was lying on her bed, eating
> pizza and drinking cola. She hadn't changed
> out of her school uniform and was still wearing
> her clunky school shoes.

My mum would go utterly crazy if I lay on my

bed with my shoes on.

Playing on the super-deluxe surround sound TV was Ruby Redfort's favourite show, 'Crazy Cops', starring Dirk Draylon, possibly the most handsome man on the planet.

There was a polite knock at the door.

"Enter," called Ruby, her mouth crammed full of pizza.

The door swung open and in glided her trusty friend and butler, Hitch.

On a silver tray was a pink and shiny telephone. It was just one of Ruby Redfort's many telephones.

"A Mr Hogtrotter for you, Miss Redfort. He's most insistent that he speaks to you."

Ruby sat up suddenly. The glass of cola fell to the floor.

She plucked up the receiver and cool as a cucumber said, "It's been a long time, Porky. I thought perhaps you'd retired."

"Not me, Miss Goody-Goody," replied the high, squeaky yet somehow sinister voice.

"So whaddya want this time? I really don't feel like a chat, I got a pizza getting cold here."

"Don't worry, I won't keep you...I just thought you might be interested to know that Dirk Draylon might not be getting so much airtime these days on account of he's working for a friend of mine...someone you ain't so keen on."

And with that the line went dead.

'It couldn't be!' thought Ruby. 'Not...' She couldn't bring herself to even think his name. 'Surely Dirk Draylon would never work for...it was unimaginable! Impossible! Out of the question!'

Ruby replaced the handset and said, "Hitch, I'll be needing my scuba gear."

I get up to switch out the light and guess what,

Grandad is tiptoeing down the garden in his indoor slippers!

He has got my torch – the rapscallion!

When he gets to the shed he opens the door and goes inside.

Is he losing his mind???

Or is he
up to something?

Whatever he is doing, it is something most definitely strange, and I am determined to get to the bottom of it, if it's the last thing I do. I have to go and switch the light on again so I can write that down in my little notebook. I wish I had one of those tiny tape-recorders like Ruby Redfort has – it makes things much easier and you don't have to keep getting up and down to turn the light on and off.

On Thursday I have swimming club.
I don't really like going – it's a bit cold.
I just go because you get crisps afterwards.

I'm not a strong swimmer –
I can't dive for a brick in pyjamas or anything.
Betty Moody can.

But I'm not sure why you need to learn to
rescue a brick while you are wearing pyjamas
because you will hardly ever find yourself
wearing pyjamas when you have to rescue
something.

It's a very rare emergency.

Betty Moody has goggles and everything and she
might become Olympic – she's got a badge.
Robert Granger can only do the doggy-paddle.
He is a splasher, and sometimes he swims with
his feet walking along the bottom.

My diving is more like falling with my arms
stretched up, but it works.
Mr Patterson says my style is technically
called a belly-flop.

Mr Patterson is a bit down in the mouth because

Betty Moody is missing swimming practise, and she is our team hopeful.

I am a bit down in the mouth because I am missing Betty Moody.

I have
no idea
where she is.

The only interesting thing that happened today was that Karl Wrenbury was chasing Toby Hawkling round the pool, trying to pull his trunks down as a joke.

But then he

f
e
l
l

in

the

d
e
e
p
end

and
started

d
r
o
w
n
i
n
g

slightly,

and Mr Patterson
had to quickly
fling
his
plimsolls
off
and dive in, in shorts!

And he said,
"That's why there is a rule which says
no monkeying around
the swimming pool!"
And,
"Next time Karl Wrenbury
might not be so lucky,
and he will be a goner."

It was very dramatic, and when I got home
I drew a picture of Karl Wrenbury nearly
drowning and sent it to my granny – she likes
to hear the news.

Before bed, I have several goes at getting into
the bathroom so I can clean my teeth.
But mysteriously there is always someone
in there.
I decide to wait outside the door, reading
my book.

Ruby plopped backwards off the speedboat and
dove down under the calm velvety black water.

She swam effortlessly. Only the bubbles from
her breathing confirmed that she was human
rather than fish.

Finally she saw it. The faint glimmer of
a light...a window.

As she approached, a circular entrance-way
slid open and Ruby glided in.

Once inside, she climbed a ladder up out of the water and into a brilliant white chamber where she changed out of her wetsuit and into dry clothes.

She was greeted by a voice on the intercom.

"Good evening, Ruby. Always a pleasure to see you, but I take it this isn't just a social call."

"No, you could say I need some help. Things have been getting pretty weird in Twinford lately and I can't help feeling it might all lead back to you-know-who."

There was a pause.

"Are you sure?"

"Well not sure, exactly, it's more of a hunch, but it has his handiwork written all over it. You know, people behaving strangely, things not quite how they oughta be. I don't know. I've just got a funny feeling that something big's gonna happen, and you know how I am with funny feelings?"

"Yes," came the voice, "you're usually right."

I wait really quite a long while, until finally the bathroom door is opened.

And guess who comes out?

Kurt.

Being in a bathroom is not at all normal for him.
My mum says Kurt can be a bit of a stranger to
hygiene. To get hygiene you must use soap
and water.

He is smelling of clean and not even
a bit like toadstools.

Friday

In the morning,
things are even
more fishy, and
I am beginning to
smell a rat.

For starters, I can't
find my hairbrush.
It is missing.

Mum is being a bit

weirdishly behaved. She lets me eat my cereal in front of the telly which is normally a NO-NO due to possible spillages, and milk is a devil to get out of upholstery.

I am pleased because it is **Dippy Dog and His Pal, Dribble.** It's an absolutely funny cartoon about a stupid dog and his friend, a rat that dribbles. I wish I had thought of that idea. Imagine thinking of that. The TV people think of so many good ideas, that's what they must do all day – think and think.

Imagine being paid to think. I would love to be in the telly business. I've got loads of ideas. I am non-non-stop thinking of things.

I could probably earn squillions a week
for my thinking.

Then the telephone goes and I overhear Mum
going, "Yes? Oh really? Oh no, what? Oh dear
heavens, I'll be right over."
Then Mum shouts, "Clarice, Minal, quick, get in
the car or you will be late for school!"
I say, "But Mum it's only 7.30 o'clock!"
She says, "Well imagine how surprised Mrs
Wilberton will be when you arrive early."
And I say, "Imagine how surprised Mrs
Wilberton will be when I arrive in my pyjamas."
And she says, "Well, you've got precisely five
seconds to find something resembling
a school uniform!"
I say, "What the Dickens is going on?"
And she says, "I haven't got time to explain,
now move it!"
I mean that was odd, wasn't it?

I arrive at school at 7.45am.

No one is there except the cleaner, who gives me a biscuit from the caretaker's cupboard.

I ask her about the mysterious incident with the coats swapping themselves over and she says that Mr Skippard had to move them all when the boys' toilets got flooded.

She said everything was in a terrible state so Mr Skippard decided to give the whole place a jolly good spring-clean.

She says, "Mr Skippard even cleaned out all the cabinets with all the school trophy cups and everything."

She says, "You name it, it's been cleaned."

I was slightly hoping for it to be more mysterious than that but I suppose it's good to have something solved.

When Mrs Wilberton sees me she says a rude comment about me actually being on time for once and that it's a shame I couldn't manage to really make her day and brush my hair.

She says, "Clarice Bean, you look like you've been dragged through a hedge backwards."
I wish someone would drag Mrs Wilberton through a hedge backwards.
She is as bad as that Mrs Drisco and I wouldn't be surprised if Patricia F Maplin Stacey didn't get the idea for Mrs Drisco from meeting Mrs Wilberton.

In class, some people are talking about their exhibits.
I am trying not to talk about mine because I am trying to keep it as top secret as possible because there might be copying from you-know-who, plus other people I could mention.
If only Betty Moody was here I could talk top secretly to her.
But she is off from school again.
No one knows where.
Grace Grapello hasn't heard my idea yet because she was luckily away when I came up with it.

I know what Bridget Garnett is doing – just the sort of project Mrs Wilberton would like.

She has chosen a book called *The Wonderful World of Oz* about Australia.

Her exhibit is going to be kangaroos and their habits.

She says she is going to spend the whole day hopping, just to see what it feels like.

Andrew Hickley is doing the same, but with wallabies.

After lunch, I am getting even more fed up with Mrs Wilberton than usual.

She says my spelling is a bit here and there, and it's interesting how I can spell the same word so many different ways.

She says, "Keep guessing and the probability is one day you will be right."

I wish I had my old teacher, Mrs Nesbit. She was really nice and she would say 'well done' just for even slightly trying.

Nowadays trying your hardest just isn't enough for some people I could mention beginning with W.

Dad always says I should just try and stay out of her way.

What I want to know is HOW, when I am in her class every single day?

I wish I was grown up.

Dad says, "It doesn't get any easier. You still have someone bossing you around."

He says he finds Mr Thorncliff, his boss, very tricky and he tries to steer clear of him as much as possible.

I say, "At least you get paid to be bossed around. I get bossed around for free."

I can't concentrate because I am busy imagining Mrs Wilberton as a hippopotamus, and I am writing:

Mrs Wilberton is a hippipotimis

Mrs Wilberton is a hippipotimis

over and over again, without really meaning to.
And what I am unaware of is that
Mrs Wilberton is standing behind
me, reading it.
She says, "Can anyone
here correctly spell
the word
hippopotamus for
Clarice Bean?"
Of course, Robert
Granger puts his
hand up which is
a joke because he is the last person who would
be able to spell hippopotamus.

Luckily for me, Mrs Marse comes
trotting in.
Mrs Marse looks a little bit like
a hedgehog in high heels.
She says, "Can Clarice Bean please
come to the secretary's office where
there is a waiting mother."

Everyone looks at me leaving because they know I must have something really important going on since I am going to miss half of an afternoon of Mrs Wilberton being dreary.

Mum is walking very fast across the playground, and I have to almost run to keep up.

When I get into the car, Minal is there chatting to himself like a twit.

Mum says, "Sorry to drag you out of class early but you would not believe the morning I have had! There will be

no one at home to let you in after school so you
are just going to have to come with me."
She says, "If it's not one thing,
it's a-blimming-nother."
I say, "Where is
Grandad? Why
isn't he at home?"
Mum says, "Grandad has got
himself into some very
deep water."
It turns out that he has
been banned from visiting his best friend
called Bert-the-Shirt Finch at the
Evergreens Old People's Home.
And that Bert-the-Shirt Finch might
be actually asked to please move out
of Evergreens as he obviously
cannot behave like a
responsible senior citizen
and abide by other
people's rules.

Until the week before last, he lived in his own flat with a Pekinese and an Alsatian, but the people in the know said he wasn't managing the stairs so well and what with one thing and another he had to be moved into an aged person's home with round-the-clock supervision.

It was for his

own good.

Bert said he didn't mind moving and that it would be nice to get his meals cooked for him. Since the only thing he was eating before was cheese on toast and sometimes just cheese on nothing.

But the slightly big problem is Evergreens Old Folk's Home is strictly no dogs allowed and absolutely no cats either.

You may have a budgie.

Mum says, "Everyone thought Bert had given his dogs to Mrs Cartwell."

But, oh no, a certain person called Grandad has

been keeping Flossie in the shed down the garden and the Pekinese called Ralph in his actual room and every night he has been smuggling them secretly into Bert's bedroom at the Evergreens.

And every morning he collects them and brings them home.

Unfortunately, Ralph escaped and chewed Mrs Perkins' budgie, Oliver, until he was actually dead.

And Mrs Perkins has lodged a complaint against Grandad and Bert, and Mum is left to pick up the pieces.

We have to wait in the corridor while Mum sorts things out for Bert and tries to get him in somewhere else where you can have a pet. Which is easier said than done.

Bert doesn't have a family, except for a long lost son in Alaska, and Mum says someone's got to come to the rescue.

Minal manages to spend 1 hour pretending to drive a toilet-roll car round the carpet. Thank goodness I have my book.

Ruby Redfort arrived back home after a long, hard day at school. Kicking off her shoes she ran upstairs to the kitchen.

Mrs Redfort was there, busying herself with whatever it was Mrs Redfort did, and Mr Redfort was reading the sporting pages.

Hitch was preparing elaborate fruit cocktails. Catching Ruby's eye, Hitch pointed discreetly at his watch. Ruby nodded.

Time was short – Hitch and Ruby were expected at headquarters at 1700 hours.

"Hi Mom, hi Dad! I just gotta go look at some history – you know, homework."

"Of course my darling, I'm glad you are paying so much attention to your studies. What are you learning about these days?" enquired her mother.

"You know, stuff," replied Ruby, evasively.

Luckily the telephone went, and Sabina Redfort became engrossed in a conversation about arranging cut flowers with Mrs Irshman.

"Quick Ruby!" whispered Hitch. "We don't have much time. I need to get you to headquarters before..."

"Oh Ruby, sweetheart..." called out her father, but Ruby was already halfway up to her room.

"See you later, Dad. Gotta study!"

"But Ruby!" continued her father. "Just to let you know, your mother and I would very much like it if you joined us for dinner this evening. Margorie and Freddy are coming over with their son, Quent. Supper will be served at eight. Ooh and sweetheart, wear something nice."

"Darn," sighed Ruby under her breath.

Apart from the nightmare of making it back in time, Quent was a real yawn.

Mr and Mrs Redfort know nothing about Hitch's life as a secret agent helper. They have no idea that being a butler is just a sideline to him.

We get home and Kurt has cooked the supper for us.

It's not too bad actually. But I can't help noticing that he has been using a hairbrush on himself. Kurt doesn't have a hairbrush! I bet he's been using mine, the weasel. I am so busy thinking about this that I almost don't notice the letter, on the table, which is addressed to me with my name on it.

I open it straight away at once.

Inside there is a postcard of Patricia F Maplin Stacey in a trouser suit. It's the same picture as on the back of every single Ruby Redfort book.

The letter says:

Dear Betty and Clarace

Thank you for your kind enquiry.
In answer to your question,
the next Ruby book will be
published this autumn.
The title is yet to be announced.

Patricia F Maplin Stacey hopes you
continue to enjoy her books and
wishes you happy reading!

Yours truly,

Patricia F Maplin Stacey
Creator of the Ruby Redfort Collection.

(Details of the fan club are listed
on the Ruby Redfort website.)

I was hoping to get a slightly more helpful
letter – it is not what I was expecting
and I don't think Patricia F Maplin Stacey
even wrote the letter herself.
It looked a bit typed and my name was spelt
wrongly and I am sure Patricia F Maplin Stacey
is a good speller.

When Dad hears all about Mum's dreadful day
he says, "It sounds like Grandad really is in the
dog-house."
Mum says, "Right now, I do not find that
remark one bit funny."

I have the whole Weekend to worry and
wonder about what has happened to
Betty Moody.
And the first thing I do is wake up at 7 o'clock
on Saturday with my mind already thinking
the worst.
One thought I had was that Mol and Cecil had

sent Betty to boarding school because I have read
about that happening to people in books when
the parents get fed up with them.
But Cecil and Mol never get fed up with Betty –
they utterly take her everywhere.
Also, Cecil and Mol have disappeared too,
and no one is answering the phone,
not even the answering machine itself.
Maybe the Moodys are on the run from the law,
or maybe Cecil has invented an invention and
someone wickedish is trying to steal it and the
Moodys have had to go into hiding.
Like in the book RUN FOR IT, RUBY.
Or maybe they have all been captured, and if
they don't hand over the secret formula they will
be dropped into a bubbling volcano, which is
what happened to Ruby Redfort in WHERE IN THE
WORLD ARE YOU, RUBY REDFORT?
In the story, it's up to Ruby's best friend, Clancy
Crew, to solve the puzzle of the missing Ruby
and follow all these clues. Clancy Crew is quite

often having to do this.

Even in this book of RUBY REDFORT RULES, I have got to this bit where Ruby seems to have disappeared, but don't worry, it's all part of her secret agent work.

Clancy Crew tried to remember all the things Ruby had said during their telephone conversation just the other night. That had been the last time Clancy had heard from Ruby. Had Ruby been trying to tell him something?

Maybe she had been captured by some arch villain and was trying to let Clancy know her whereabouts in some sort of code. Now Clancy thought of it, it did seem strange that Ruby had mentioned that she was having tapioca pudding in China. Ruby Redfort hated tapioca pudding – everybody knew that! And just what was she doing in China?

In the story, Clancy does some quick thinking and works out tapioca stands for BAD NEWS (because tapioca is bad news if you don't like it) 'in' just stands for IN and China stands for City Help I Need Advice.

So the message is:

…BAD NEWS. IN CITY. HELP! I NEED ADVICE…

It's so clever, I wish I knew code.

I get a sort of clue when I go downstairs.

It's come through the letter-box.

It's a postcard with a picture of a strange, curly-shaped building on it and the words

Wish you were here!

The corner is torn off and I can't read who it is from.

Of course, it could be from Betty because there is a B and it is written in Betty's handwriting.

Maybe she is probably trying to tell me something…

but what?

I run to show Mum, but she is busy chatting
to Kurt.
That may not seem odd to you but
if you know him, you know
Kurt never just chats.

On
Sunday
I go over
to my friend
Alexandra Holker's.
She is eating pizza
and she tells me what
happened at school after I
had to leave for the emergency.

What she says is that Toby Hawkling and Karl Wrenbury told Mrs Wilberton they were doing the dictionary as their book exhibit.

And Mrs Wilberton said something like, "What an awfully good idea indeed."

And Toby Hawkling said, "We are going to write down lots of words and print them up really giantly and stick them in the corridor."

Mrs Wilberton said, "Well, for once, Karl Wrenbury and Toby Hawkling, I actually approve."

Unfortunately, she changed her mind when she saw the words they had chosen.

She said, "Well, if you two like words so much, I have got just the thing for you."

She kept them in all break.

She made them write:

I am not big and I am not clever

over and over again, for at least a hundred times.

She says, "They are not to be in a pair because they can't conduct themselves like mature,

grown-up children, and that one of them
is always egging the other one on and that
they just spend their valuable learning time
being silly."

She said, "If they can't behave like decent little
boys, then too bad, they won't be treated like
decent little boys."

She said, "I won't have it! Do you hear me?
I won't have it!"

Monday

I thought it was quite funny, until today when
Mrs Wilberton says, "Since Betty has decided
not to bother to come to school for the past
few days, Clarice Bean can join up with
Karl Wrenbury."

Of course, I am utterly speechless.

To make matters worse, when a certain person
beginning with G called Grace Grapello finds
out that I am allowed to do Ruby Redfort, she
says that she is too and that it was her idea all

along and it is me that is copying her. And that she is going to do a Ruby Redfort exhibit.

Mrs Wilberton says, "Absolutely no way, hozay!" Then she says, "In fact I am not even sure anyone is going to be doing an exhibit based on such drivel."

Mrs Wilberton starts being very critical of my idea.

She says, "The Ruby Redfort series is not a good example of the literature of our times."

How can she say this?????

I say one of my ideas is to make badges because Ruby's got these great phrases which she says a lot and they would make good badges and people could wear them.

Things like:

That's my name, don't wear it out.

Beat it, buster!

Take that, scumbo!

and

You're an armpit.

Mrs Wilberton says Ruby Redfort has got an unpleasant turn of phrase and is unsuitable material for little girls.

She says, "These books are encouraging girls to run wild and I would prefer it if you picked a new project…

…how about ballet dancing?"

She says, "If you will insist on doing this Redfort book, you will have to go and talk to Mr Pickering. Maybe he can talk some sense into you."

Mr Pickering says, "I think it is fine to do the Ruby books as your exhibit, because enjoying reading is important. I'm all for it.

However, part of the book exhibit is about choosing a book that you have learnt something from. And you can only have a chance of winning the cup and the mystery prize if you can tell everybody what that is."

Mr Pickering says he is very much looking forward to seeing what I come up with.

He says he has bought the Ruby Redfort books for his niece and that he wishes he had time to read them himself – they sound very exciting.

And I say,

"They are."

I come out of Mr Pickering's office and there is Grace Grapello, doing her sneering face and she says something like, "Copycat."

And I say,

"It is you that is copying me and you know it."

And she says, "Liar!"

And I say, "Big bum!"

Grace Grapello is my arch enemy. The reason she is my worst person at school, apart from Mrs Wilberton, is because she is such a know-it-all and she is always annoying me with annoying comments and she can be really a meany.

Once she invited Betty Moody to her birthday skating party without asking me.

She isn't even a friend of Betty Moody's.

Betty said, "No thank you, Grace. I am going to tea with my utterly best friend, Clarice Bean."

And that was that, and that is why Betty Moody is my absolutely best friend.

Mum says, "I am afraid you will always bump into girls like Grace Grapello.

I remember at my school there was a nasty piece of work called Felicity Marchmont.

She used to put chewing-gum in my gym shoes and tell people I had fleas."

Mum says the only way to deal with girls like Felicity is to feel sorry for them.

They must be very sad people if the only pleasure they get is making other people absolutely not like them.

I say, "I can't feel sorry for Grace Grapello because she is too
utterly horrible."

Mum says, "Fair enough, then just picture her as a slug."

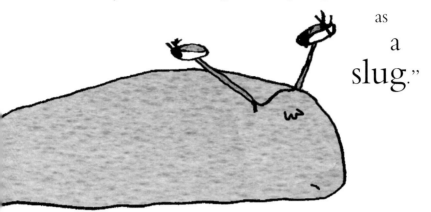

When I get back to class I have to think really hard about what is going to be the learning part of my exhibit.

I am sure there is lots of learning in the Ruby Redfort books.

There must be because they are about someone really clever and it is written by someone really clever.

So it means I must have learnt something, but what?

During break I do a bit more reading of

RUBY REDFORT RULES to see if I can quickly learn something.

Ruby rounded the corner and ran straight into her arch enemy, Vapona Begwell, who was hanging out by the water fountain, talking to her friend, Gemma Melamare.

They were discussing the school election and who was going to be voted Class President.

"Just so long as it isn't that Ruby Redfort kid, then, win or lose, I really couldn't care," sneered Vapona.

"Oh you are going to win for sure, Vapona," replied Gemma, patting her friend on the back.

"Hey Gem, can you smell a funny smell?" said the gravelly-voiced Vapona, pretending to sniff the air, "Oh, hi Ruby, there you are."

"Hi bugwart," replied Ruby. "Did you take a look in the mirror lately? You seem to have something weird on your face – oh no, my mistake, it's just your nose."

After school, Karl Wrenbury comes up to me
and says he doesn't want to do
a **stupid** girls' book
about a **stupid girl,**
and that it will be really
stupid and boring.
I say, "Oh really!
So it is stupid to be an undercover secret agent
and to rescue people using just your wits and
some new-fangled gadgets is it?
And I suppose fighting arch evil-doers and flying
about in a purplish helicopter is boring to
someone like you who only comes to school on
a little bike."
And I say, "For your information, they are going
to make it into a Hollywood movie."
I can tell he's quite impressed.
And once I have told him about the slimeball,
Hogtrotter, arch rapscallion, and I have happened
to mention about how the evil Count von
Viscount tries to drop Ruby Redfort and Clancy

Crew into a bubbling volcano, but Hitch rescues them in exactly the nick of time, then he is suddenly quite keen.

He says he isn't so interested in the rescuing bit, but the rest of it is quite good.

I lend him one of my Ruby books called WHERE IN THE WORLD ARE YOU, RUBY REDFORT?

He has to promise not to let his dog chew it.

Then I show Karl the postcard of the curly buildings, which all clues point to being from Betty Moody, and he says she has probably been kidnapped by aliens who want to take over the world.

This is just the sort of thing I was afraid of.

So, when I get home I call Granny and she gets me to describe the picture.

She doesn't say anything for a couple of minutes and there is a strange choking sound.

And then Granny says, in a slightly strange, whispery voice, "I'm sorry, I've just swallowed a mint humbug. I will have to call you back."

When she does she says, "It sounds very much to me as if our friend Betty is in Russia."

On Tuesday, Grace Grapello and Cindy Fisher say they are going to do the history of ballet. They have chosen a book called *Dance Magic*.

Mrs Wilberton looks utterly pleased. This is exactly the type of book project that she would love.

She says, "Well girls, I very much look forward to seeing what you do because ballet is a personal passion of mine."

Grace Grapello looks at me with a slimy smile, which makes me want to be slightly sick.

Mrs Wilberton tells Toby Hawkling he has to go in their group.

He does not look so pleased.

Later when I tell Granny, she says, "Grace Grapello is obviously completely desperate and will stop at nothing to win."

It's weird but Karl Wrenbury actually has some quite good ideas.

He says he is working on something at home which he says means we will most likely win the competition and we will get the little cup with our names on which everyone will see, including Grace Grapello.

Toby Hawkling is being a nuisance and trying to put Karl off.

He says, "Ha ha ha, you are doing a girls' book."

And Karl says, "So what. You are doing ballet."

Toby Hawkling creeps back to his desk.

I invite Karl over after school but he says he is up to his ears making a scene from Ruby Redfort.

But he will just come over for maybe an hour and a quarter.

He is dreadfully busy.

He's doing a model of the volcano where Count von Viscount is about to finish Ruby Redfort and Clancy Crew off, and Count von Viscount says, "Farewell, you meddling kids!" and then he does this chilling laugh.

And Karl is going to do a recording of a chilling laugh and play it over and over on a tiny tape-recorder.

He just needs to find a chilling laugh so he can tape it.

Not as easy as you might think.

He says he thinks Ruby Redfort isn't so bad, considering it's just a girls' book.

I say, "Ruby Redfort is not just a girls' book, it's an everyone book. Mr Pickering himself is going to read them."

Later at my house, Karl Wrenbury is actually being quite incredibly funny.

He can make his eyes go in different directions both at the same time.

He says he will teach my brother, Minal, how to do it if he wants.

And he can drink orange juice through a straw
up his nose.

When I tell Mum she says this is extraordinary
but not necessarily something to do at the dinner
table.

I say, "But you should see it, it is utterly
amazing."

Mum says she enjoys the weird and wonderful
but she doesn't feel the need to see orange
juice go up Karl Wrenbury's nose.

Karl says when he is old enough
he will grow a beard and
have at least
six dogs.
After Karl goes,
I am thinking
how it would
be utterly
good if
Betty Moody
came back.

She would really like Karl Wrenbury,
I am sure of it.
Betty and me find completely the same things
funny.
If my mother and father were rich and had
a butler who could fly a helicopter, then I could
buzz over there and collect Betty back from
Russia.
Ruby's father, Mr Redfort is rich because he is
a multi-millionaire and Mrs Redfort is a lady
who lunches, which means she doesn't do
anything except get her hair washed
professionally and have her nails painted in a
beauty salon, then she goes to meet her friends
for lunch and she says things like, "Darling, how
simply divine to see you," and then she comes
home and gets changed into an evening-gown
and goes out for dinner.
And that is simply all she does.
I say, "Mum, how come you don't change into
an evening-gown for dinner?"

She says, "I do, it's called a dressing-gown, now hurry up and get those baked beans down you smartish!"

My life is nothing like Ruby Redfort's.

On Wednesday, me and Karl are working on our exhibit.

It's going to be really good.

I'm sure of it.

Toby Hawkling asks Mrs Wilberton if he can join in with us if he absolutely promises to be strictly properly behaved.

Mrs Wilberton says, "Not on your nelly, Toby Hawkling." Then she laughs.

I don't like it when Mrs Wilberton laughs – it gives me the shivers.

Karl is thinking of lots of gadgets and things we can make, and all I have to do is borrow my dad's electrical shaver and my mum's powder-puffing case, the toaster and a few other whatnots, and then Karl says he can make them into Ruby Redfort special zappers and walkie-talkies and transmitters and all kinds of other clever things like that.

I don't know how Karl Wrenbury knows all this because I don't.

He says his dad used to help him before he went off somewhere.

He never came back.

But before that happened they made lots of useful things together.

Now Karl does them on his own, in the shed.

It's lucky Karl is so clever because Mum is too busy down the community centre to help.

She says everyone will have to get their own tea and things because she is still helping Bert find a new place to live.

I know this is important, but so is a cardigan with jam on it needing a wash.

Mum says, "Get Grandad to show you how to use the machine."

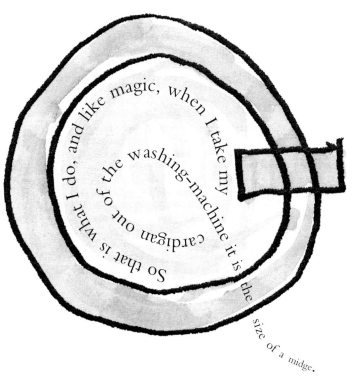

So that is what I do, and like magic, when I take my cardigan out of the washing-machine it is the size of a midge.

Domestics aren't really Grandad's strong point –
not anymore,
not with everything being all technology and
everything.
In the old days, washing meant two hands and
a bar of soap and then rubbing.
I have to clean the washbasin,
that is one of my jobs.
Can you imagine Ruby Redfort cleaning the
washbasin?
The answer is NO because she has Mrs Digby
who looks after her every need.
Ruby Redfort is too busy solving crime to clean
a washbasin.
Mum says if I moan about this she will get me to
clean the toilet.
I'm thinking about calling the child protector
people.

The difference between my parents and Ruby's
parents is Ruby's mother and father give Ruby

everything she needs,
        which is most things.
                And
        my parents
                don't.

Once I have done my cleaning, I go to my
room.
I am trying to be alone so I can do some
thinking and work out some answers to some
big questions.
But the little squirt, Minal, comes barging in
and as usual is babbling on about nonsense.
The advantage of being an only child is you
could have a room of your own and not be
bugged by nincompoops.
Also, I would be more likely to get extra
pocket-money so I can send off for the new
Ruby Redfort underwater lie detector watch
which is 24.99 pounds!
You can get someone to wear it and it will tell

you if they are lying because when they are lying
their pulse starts to beat really fast and then the
watch beeps!

Betty says it doesn't really work if they have
been running because then your pulse always
beats really fast.

And then you have to ask yourself,

'Have they been running,

or are they lying and it might be that they are
lying about having been running?'

But how do you know that?

Betty also says it leaks underwater.

Anyway, it's great because it has this picture of
Ruby Redfort in the middle, and the actual
hands of the watch come out of her nose,
and the second hand is a
fly.

The other thing I am wondering about is Betty,
and that maybe she is just in Russia on a holiday
and not kidnapped by aliens, and if she is just on

holiday, why didn't she bother to even tell me she was going?

Ruby Redfort was sitting in her special thinking chair on the roof.

Mrs Digby had made her a super multivitamin drink to help her brain think faster.

While she sipped, she inspected her latest gadget. Control had given it to her when she was summoned to HQ.

The gadget turned out to be rather interesting. It was a tiny backpack that folded out to form a pair of wings just big enough for an eleven-year-old girl. They were a new design, straight from the lab. It meant if Ruby ever got trapped in a tight spot, high up, say, on top of a building, she could just jump off and glide safely down. Who knew when she might need to do that?

At school, on
Thursday,
I can't quite believe
it because guess
who has
appeared out of
nowhere? Betty
Moody, and she
is wearing a hat
with earflaps.
She says she has been
in Russia because her
mum, Call-Me-Mol,
had a book
launching do,
and at the
absolutely last minute
Mol and Cecil
thought, 'What could
be better than to
take Betty?'

Betty said that one hardly ever gets to go to
Russia, and that is why, if someone asks you if
you want to go,

you must say,

utterly
yes.

I can't wait to tell Betty about the book exhibit.
I say, "Guess what our book exhibit is going
to be?"
I don't wait for her to guess,
I just say, "Ruby Redfort, arch detective!"
Betty says it's a brilliant idea.
And of course, she is right.
Betty says everyone is reading Ruby Redfort in
Russia too, and that in Russian she is called
something more Russian.
And then Betty says,
"You will never believe it but guess who I met
in Russia?
Patricia F Maplin Stacey!"
And she's right – I don't believe it.

And then Betty shows me a picture of herself
standing next to Patricia F Maplin Stacey.
Which is proof that it is true.
Patricia F Maplin Stacey looks nothing like
the picture of herself on the back cover.
She is much older and she is not wearing
a trouser suit.

She is shorter
than she is
meant to be.
And Betty says,
"Yes, that is
the strange
thing."
Betty says
I must come
back for tea
because she
has got a
present from
Russia for me.

I utterly can't wait, but then I remember about how I am supposed to be meeting up with Karl to work on our exhibit.

When I tell Betty she says, "But why are you paired up with Karl Wrenbury?

You are meant to be in a pair with me."

And then I tell her about how it was Mrs Wilberton and not me who came up with that idea and that I didn't even want to be doing an exhibit with Karl Wrenbury but that it turns out that he is quite good at ideas and that it turns out that he is quite nice and you might not think he would be.

But he is.

Betty says, "But Karl Wrenbury is always being stupid and he will mess everything up."

I say, "But he has come up with some utterly amazing gadgets.

He really has.

And I think you would

really like him.

He is utterly funny
and he can drink orange juice up his nose!"
Betty says,
"Oh well,
if you like Karl Wrenbury so much
then you can do your stupid Ruby
exhibit with him."
I can't believe what she is saying. Betty
Moody would never call Ruby Redfort stupid.
I say,
"Well you're the one who
just went off
and didn't even bother to tell me
you were going."
And she says,
"I jolly well did tell you!
I left two messages!
And one message
was from a telephone
in actual
Russia!"

And I shout,
"Oh yes?
Well how come
I didn't get them?"
And she shouts,
"Well ask your brother, Kurt,
and your grandad because
I most certainly did leave messages
and they will tell you
that it's true.
And I sent you a postcard
from Russia!
And maybe I shouldn't have
bothered!"
And then Mrs Wilberton shouts,
"Will you two please pipe down!
We do not tolerate
shouting
at this school."
I want to tell her that she herself is shouting,
but I decide not to.

Betty won't talk to me for all the rest of the day.
We have never had an even slightest argument before.
Except for once when I ate her packed lunch doughnut by accident.
I can't believe it.
It's the most awfullest thing that has ever happened in my whole utter entire life.
I am walking home on my own, filled with gloom.
And I am thinking about the postcard which was – just as I thought – from Betty, and about the message which I found Cement, our dog, eating which must have been from Betty.
And the message my grandad couldn't remember properly, and that was of course from Betty when she was actually in Russia.
And she is right –
she did try to tell me.

I try to read RUBY REDFORT RULES just to cheer

myself up but I am feeling almost too full of a gloomy feeling.

"Jeepers, Ruby! What do ya s'pose happened here?"

Ruby Redfort and Clancy Crew were looking at the wreckage that used to be Mr Crew's study.

His safe had been broken into and all the important top secret documents it had once contained were gone.

"Looks like you've been burgled," sighed Ruby. "Reckon they found what they were looking for?"

"Never mind what they took, what do you suppose this is doing here?"

Clancy Crew was just staring. He didn't know what to think.

He was holding a jacket. It wasn't any old jacket, it was the one that Dirk Draylon always wore in 'Crazy Cops'.

"Dirk Draylon couldn't have done this, could he Ruby? I mean he wouldn't would he?"

"Nah, I don't think so, Clance. Something's wrong about all this, you know what I mean? I smell a big fat rat. I'll bet you a million milkshakes this is a set-up. Someone just wants us to think Dirk Draylon is involved. Oh boy, do I smell a rat."

On Friday, Mrs Wilberton has a very livid look on her face and says she has just about had it up to here.
She says this time she means business.
I am really wondering what she is
on about, and also how she
manages to make her eyes go
so beady.
And I am thinking how she
could almost be the evil
Count von Viscount,
in disguise.

They have the same eyebrows, I am sure of it...
I am remembering that bit in **RUBY REDFORT SAVES THE DAY**, when Ruby is at the ambassador's very important party and there is this old lady there who seems entirely innocent and not remotely dodgy.

And then Ruby Redfort gets one of her suspicions about her and pulls off the lady's face, which is a mask, only to find that it is really Count von Viscount, who is of course livid to be discovered and maybe it is the same with Mrs Wilberton. Maybe if I...

"Clarice Bean, you seem to be looking very shifty, perhaps you would like to tell us all what's on your mind?"

Of course I don't think it would be a good idea to tell Mrs Wilberton that she has the eyebrows of a wicked count.

So I just look sheepish.

Mrs Wilberton says, "Clarice Bean, I am really
not prepared to tell you again, if you cannot be
bothered to pay attention to me, then maybe you
will pay attention to Mr Pickering!"

I wait outside Mr Pickering's office for maybe
approximately 23 minutes.

I am starting to know how it must feel to be
Karl Wrenbury.

I am just staring at a poster which says

DANGERS IN THE HOME

and then has a picture of a lady standing on
a rickety stool, changing a light bulb, while she
is being distracted by a small baby, who is
playing with a pair of scissors.

Karl Wrenbury must have looked at this poster
a lot.

Finally, Mrs Marse says, "Mr Pickering is
occupied with important business. He will not
have time to tell you off."

So I go back to my classroom.

What Mrs Wilberton is up in arms about is that,
"Someone, and I've got a pretty good idea who
you are, has stolen the book exhibit winners'
cup."
Karl Wrenbury is instantly sent home!
Mrs Wilberton says it must be him because, quite
frankly, it always is.
And also, he was seen loitering around the glass
trophy cupboard where the cup is always kept.
And now it is missing and you don't have to
be a genius to work out what happened.
Mrs Wilberton says Karl will not be allowed
to take part in the competition because he has
reached a level of naughtiness which will not
be tolerated.
I am utterly beside myself because now I might
be disqualified from the competition.
And I have lost two exhibit partners in a row.
And if I am not careful, I will end up being in
a pair with Toby Hawkling.

I have an utterly drearily and miserablish
weekend because my best friend, Betty
Moody, is not being best friends with me
anymore.

And when I go over to Karl Wrenbury's house
he says he can't be bothered to finish the Ruby
model since he is disqualified.

Karl Wrenbury says, "It's not fair because I didn't
even do it."

I say, "Oh really?"

He says, "Why would I steal the cup when
I thought we were going to win it?"

Quite a good point actually.

The other thing is, Karl Wrenbury never says
he hasn't done something bad because he is
utterly proud of his wicked ways.

So he is obviously not the culprit.

All I know is, now I am definitely not going
to win.

I have no Ruby gadgets, only half of a not-
finished model and, for a start, I can't think of

a learning thing to do with our exhibit.

I haven't even made my Ruby badges and they were going to be utterly popular.

I am thinking about giving up.

When I get back home, I telephone my granny.

I tell her all about the missing cup and how Karl most likely didn't do it and is in deep troubling water for a crime he didn't commit, and that everything is

dreadfully suspicious

and

utterly wrong.

I say, "It just doesn't add up, Granny."

Which is exactly what Ruby Redfort would say if she had to solve this crime.

And Granny says, "If Karl didn't do it then somebody else must have, and the big question is who?"

I say, "Yes, who?"

And Granny says, "Mrs Pinkerton!"

I say, "Who's Mrs Pinkerton? I don't think there's

anyone called Mrs Pinkerton at my school?"
And Granny says, "No, no. I am meant to be
over, playing cards, at Mrs Pinkerton's – I'm
late!"
She says, "I will have to go, but Clarice, maybe
you could solve the mystery."
I say,

"But how can I?
I'm not a
mystery solver."
Granny says, "You must have learnt something
about solving a mystery after reading all those
Ruby Redfort detective books.
Let me know how you get on."

I sit for ages thinking about what Granny has
just said, and the more I think about it, the more
I think she is right.
I must have learnt lots about being a mystery
solver from Ruby Redfort, and if I can solve
this mystery, then I can prove Karl Wrenbury

is not the cup stealer.

And if I can prove he is not the cup stealer, then I can prove that I have learnt something from reading the Ruby Redfort books which Mrs Wilberton likes to call drivel, when in fact they are packed with good advice and clever useful information.

I nip straight upstairs.

The first thing is, you have to make a list.

That's what Ruby always does.

She has a special tiny computer to write on.

But it is not utterly necessary to have one, which I don't.

Also, you do not need a magnifying glass, because that is old-fashioned.

Just your wits and a biro and a smallish piece of paper.

Then you write down all the clues.

The most important clues are the people you are suspicious about.

They are called the suspects.
My mainly suspects would be
Mrs Wilberton and Grace Grapello.
Mrs Wilberton probably didn't do it,
even though I would like it to be her.
All evidence points to it being Grace
Grapello because she is probably highly
jealous of our idea and desperate to

have a good one of her own, but can't.
Toby Hawkling is my thirdish suspect,
it's always good to have three people
on your list.
Three is normal for suspects.
Robert Granger isn't a suspect
because he would never have
thought of it.
He never thinks of anything on his
own without copying someone else
and also he is a goody-goody.

The other thing I have to write down is
just when did they find the cup was missing????
No one has seen it in the glass trophy cupboard
since Mr Skippard did his spring-clean-up.
So for all anybody knows, it could have been
stolen before, when the boys' toilets got flooded,
over nearly two weeks ago.
This starts me thinking, and then I get stuck, so
I do a bit more reading.

Ruby Redfort was thinking hard.

What did it all mean? She felt this might be
a good time to talk things over with her good
friend, Clancy Crew. Clancy had a way of
figuring things out.

He was very bright.

She dialled the number.

"Hi Clance, how you doing?"

"Is that you Ruby? I was hoping you would
call. I am stuck here at this boring dinner. My
dad is entertaining all these celebrities and

government people and boy is it a yawn."

Clancy Crew's father was ambassador and was always inviting very important, top-notch guests for dinner. He liked to come across as a family man and insisted that all five of his children always attend these social functions.

"Do you think you might be able to slip away?" asked Ruby.

"Not a chance. Could you maybe make it over here?"

It was Hitch's night off, and there was no one to drive her over to Clancy's house, but that was OK, she could ride her bike.

Of course, Ruby Redfort's bike was no ordinary bike and was fitted with a phone, a rocket-booster and an anti-attack repeller.

"I'll be there in five," said Ruby, and climbed out of her bedroom window.

The person I really want to talk to is Betty
Moody but she isn't talking to me.

I tell Mum how
    everything is ruined,
and that Betty and me are
        not utterly best friends
anymore.

And how it will never be the same again.
                       Never not ever.

Mum says, "I think you are being a little
bit dramatic.

If Betty isn't talking to you then maybe you
should go and talk to her.

Real friends don't let some tiny little argument
get in the way.

If they did then no one would be talking
to anybody."

She says, "Why don't you see if Betty would
like to come over for tea?

We might have sausages."

I walk very slowly because I feel a bit sick – I am anxiously worrying that Betty Moody will shut the front door in my face.

I ring the doorbell. It's not a normal doorbell of course.

The Moodys brought it back from the Far East.

It is made of wood tubes and makes a woody sound.

Our doorbell only works from time to time – you never know when.

Betty Moody herself actually answers the door.

She is wearing furry slipper boots.

I expect they are Russian.

She says, "Hello, Clarice Bean,"
as if nothing is wrong, although she is fidgeting quite a bit.

I say, "Hello, Betty, would you like to come over for tea?

We will be probably having sausages."

Betty says, "Will Karl Wrenbury be there?"

I say, "Utterly no."
Betty says, "Alright, I'll come over at six."
Then I go home feeling slightly a bit better.
Although I notice she doesn't give me my
present from Russia.

When I get home, I almost get knocked over
in my own hallway by the several dogs we
now have.

They are barking like mad, and Mum says she
is at her wits' end.
Dad says he has never felt so keen to go back
to work in his life.
Mum says Grandad had better find somewhere
to put them all, i.e. not in this house.
I go into the kitchen,
and there is Chloë Brownling.
She is one of Marcie's friends, which is odd
because Marcie is out and not here and it is
just Kurt and Chloë on their own,
with each other
alone.
Sittingawfully
closely.
And Kurt
is making her a
cup of herbally tea,

and he is talking and saying things like,
"Would you like a buttered crumpet?" and,
"I like your hair that way,
it really suits you."
Of course, I am astonished.
When I tell Mum about it she says, "Yes, Chloë
is Kurt's new girlfriend.
I think he really likes her."
She says, "Kurt is a lot better now he has
a reason to wash, but Marcie is worse than ever."
Mum says, "Marcie isn't talking to Kurt because
she feels Kurt has stolen her friend.
And Kurt isn't talking to Marcie because Marcie
told Chloë that Kurt's room smells of cheese."
Which is true.
Mum says, "For goodness sake! Why can't
people just get along?"

When Chloë sees Flossie, who is of course an
Alsatian, she screams like a maniac which just
makes things utterly worse.

All of the dogs start loudly barking.

And Chloë says she can't come round anymore
because she is utterly terrified of Alsatians.

And isn't really a dog person, full stop.

Kurt goes into a decline.

He says, "I hate living here sometimes."

Dad says, "I know how you feel, this house
is going to the dogs."

Mum gives him a look.

Then Mrs Stampney comes over.

She is in curlers and fed up to the back teeth.

She says she is trying to have a relaxing bath
but it is hard to relax when there are three
howling dogs on the other side of the wall.

She says this is a disturbance to the peace and her
nerves are literally frayed.

She says she is making a complaint to the police
station about us.

Mum says she would be quite happy to drive her
round there.

Then the doorbell goes and it is Karl Wrenbury.

He says, "Sit!" and all the dogs sit, and he says,
"Quiet!" and all the dogs are quiet.

He says he has dogs at home, and he spends most
of his time training them.

His mum is a dog walker, and he has learnt quite
a bit about dog obedience.

Mum says she is very grateful
and would he like to stay for
tea? We are having sausages.
And Karl says, "Yes, please."
But of course, it is an
utter disaster when
I remember that Betty
Moody is coming over.
What will she say when
she sees Karl
Wrenbury? She might
never forgive me.
At that moment,
the doorbell goes.

It only goes slightly PING because it has lost the
PONG bit, which is a pity.

Ruby Redfort has a doorbell which plays a tune.

When I open the door it's Betty Moody.

She sees the dogs and she goes utterly
over the moon.

Betty Moody loves dogs but the Moodys can
never ever have one because they are always
leaving the
country at the
drop of a hat.
And you can't
just take a dog
with you whenever
you feel like it.
Which I suppose is why
we never go
anywhere.

Karl shows Betty how to make them sit and beg.
He says, if she wants, she can come over and
walk his dogs sometimes after school.
Mum says, "You are welcome to borrow
these two if you want to see what it's like to
own some."
She is joking but Betty phones Mol and Cecil
anyway and asks them if she can look after
Flossie and Ralph, just for one, maybe two
weeks until Bert can find a new old folks' home
which is equipped for taking pets.
And Mol says it might be very good for Betty
to experience the responsibility of looking after
an animal.
And so the answer is maybe yes.
Mum says, "Thank goodness for that."
Kurt goes to call Chloë and Betty decides Karl
isn't so bad after all.

On Monday, back at school, Karl and Betty
are chattering non-stop about dogs.

Betty seems to have forgotten all about not liking Karl Wrenbury and calling him a super limpet. When I ask her, she says she never didn't like him, she just didn't want him messing everything up for us and our exhibit.

She says, "If he is going to be a helpful influence then he can certainly be in our pair."

The only problem is Karl is not allowed to do the exhibit because he is still

in trouble

for stealing the little cup.

And although I have been working on a gadget thingy of my own, Karl was doing the best bit of the exhibit, and I am worried it is going to be rubbish without him.

Betty says, "In any case, we can't win the competition if we can't think of anything that we have learnt from Ruby Redfort.

And that's the problem, we can't."

I say, "But that is what I have been meaning to tell you.

I think we can solve the crime and win the cup
because it turns out that we have learnt quite
a lot from Ruby Redfort."

I tell Betty Moody what my plan is and she says
she 'will definitely help'.
And 'wow, how exciting.'
We are interviewing everyone
about what they know,
and what they don't know,
and what they don't know they know.
That's something that Clancy Crew always says.
He says, "Sometimes people don't even know
what they know because they haven't really
thought about it. But if they did, they would
realise they knew more than they thought
they knew."
I think I know what he means.
We ask Alexandra Holker.
I say we are investigating the missing cup … and
when exactly it did go missing,

i.e. maybe it was stolen just after the boys' toilets got flooded.

And Alexandra says, "You know what, Clarice Bean, I think you might be on to something."

Which is weird because that's just what Clancy Crew would say.

I ask her what she thinks about the culprit perhaps being Grace Grapello.

And she says, "Well, the thing is, Grace Grapello was away with a germy-flu bug and so was not there when we think the actual little cup went missing."

Of course she is right.

I say, "What about Toby Hawkling, do you think he did it?"

And Alexandra says, "No, not really, because Toby Hawkling never does anything without Karl Wrenbury telling him to."

And of course, she is right.

I say, "What about Mrs Wilberton, do you think she stole the cup?"

And she says, "No."

I say, "What makes you think that?"

And she says, "Because she is the teacher."

Alexandra Holker would be a really good
detective because she has a really good memory
for details and that is a must if you are going to
be a detective.

So if it's not Mrs Wilberton, and not Grace
Grapello, and not Toby Hawkling, just who is it?
We can't think of anyone, and all our clues are
adding up to make one big zero, which is what
Ruby says sometimes to her butler, Hitch.

And what Hitch often says is, "Sometimes you
just have to look at things

sideways

and then

you get

a clearer picture."

I'm not sure what that means, but when we get
back to the Moodys' house we ask Mol and she
says, "I think what Hitch means is, if you think
about something in a different way then
sometimes its easier to find the answer."
She says, "What you have to think about is why
would anyone steal the cup in the first place?
There's no point having the winners' cup
if it doesn't have your name written on it
saying
'Winner'
and there's no point having it at all if you can't
show it to everybody at the open day."
She says, "Maybe if you think about the cup
as being lost rather than stolen, then just
perhaps, you might find it."
Mol is really clever at these things because she
is a crime writer.
Her whole life is about puzzling things out.

On Tuesday,
Betty Moody and I are
busy searching for the cup.
We look everywhere,
even outside in the giant bins
with wheels.
We give up after Betty nearly falls
in. We have to get Mr Skippard to
rescue Betty's glasses, which have
unfortunately slipped off her nose,
into the rubbish.
Mr Skippard is quite cross and says
he has better things to do than climb
in and out of dustbins.
He says if it happens again, he will
have a good mind to confiscate
Betty Moody's glasses and keep them
in his cupboard.
Mr Skippard wouldn't really do that
because he is not as mean as he wants
you to think he is.

But it gives me a good idea.

You see, one of the places we haven't looked is in Mr Skippard's actual cupboard of cleaning equipment, and the cup could maybe perhaps have got in there by accident when Mr Skippard was having his spring-clean-up.

Betty says, "It's a long shot, but it's worth a try." Which is what Clancy Crew says in every single story.

Very unfortunately indeed, Betty Moody and me get caught redhanded, clattering about in Mr Skippard's cupboard.

Mr Skippard is definitely extremely cross.

He says, "The caretaker's cupboard is absolutely off-limits and totally out of bounds for all pupils. And that is final."

Even more utterly unfortunately, Mrs Wilberton is passing by when Mr Skippard is telling us off and then we are in big trouble.

Mrs Wilberton says, "Well, Clarice Bean, I am not so surprised by this wilfully disgraceful lack of good conduct." Whatever that means.

"But as for you, Betty Moody, I am sorry but I really thought you had more sense."

She says, "Well since the two of you like cupboards so much, you can both stay in during break and stack

    all the

        books

        in

MY cupboard."

Of course, this is a nuisance because we are trying to solve a mystery.

And we have got more important things to do than sort things out for someone beginning with W who is too lazy to clear up her own cupboard.

It takes ages because we are taking it in turns to read RUBY REDFORT RULES out loud to each other.

After negotiating her way through countless winding corridors, and climbing endless flights of stone stairs, Ruby Redfort arrived at a steel door. She felt certain that this must be the door behind which the unfortunate celebrity was held.

Ruby picked the lock without much difficulty, and there, looking just a little bemused, was Dirk Draylon.

"Boy, am I glad to see you," sighed Dirk. "I didn't think I was ever gonna get outta here."

"Don't worry, Dirk. I'll get you out," whispered Ruby as she untied the weary TV star.

"You take my glider wings. They are only designed to take the weight of an eleven-year-old girl, but you look like you've lost a lot of pounds, Dirk, and hey, we don't have much choice."

"But what about you?"

"Don't worry about me, Dirk, I'll be just fine."

"I owe you big time, kid," he said, before jumping from the tiny window and floating the 200-and-something metres to the ground below.

It was at that moment Ruby heard a chilling voice behind her.

"So we meet again, Ruby Redfort — arch interferer and tiresome schoolgirl. You really think you can outwit the evil genius, Count von Viscount, do you?"

"Well, I thought I would give it a go," joked Ruby, trying to sound relaxed although her heart was beating so fast she could barely breathe.

"Well, since you are here, I might as well tell you my little idea. It's incredibly clever."

Betty is reading away when I accidentally knock something off the shelf I am tidying, and it hits her on the head.

You'll utterly **never** believe it, but it's the tiny cup.

What is it doing in Mrs Wilberton's cupboard is what I want to know.

Just then, Mrs Wilberton calls out, "Clarice Bean, Betty, will you please come out of that cupboard and sit down."

And I say, "Mrs Wilberton, I didn't know that there were two cups for the book exhibit winners."

And she says, "Well, that is because there aren't."

I say, "But Mrs Wilberton, there's a little cup in your cupboard and it looks just exactly like the little cup for the winner of the exhibit.

You know, like the little cup that Karl Wrenbury has stolen."

And when Mrs Wilberton sees the cup she goes as red as an actual beetroot, and then she beetles off to see Mr Pickering.

She doesn't come back for ages.

It turns out Mrs Wilberton asked Mr Skippard to give the cup a bit of a polish-up to get it

ready for the open day evening. She said to put
it safely in the cupboard, but there was a mix-up
because Mr Skippard thought Mrs Wilberton meant
safely in her classroom cupboard since she would be
needing it on this actual Wednesday, but Mrs
Wilberton meant safely in the glass trophy cupboard.

On my way out of school, I hear Mrs Marse say,
"Mr Pickering was absolutely livid and said to
Mrs Wilberton that she cannot go around blaming
people willy-nilly for things they didn't do."
And then Mr Skippard said, "I couldn't agree
more."

Betty comes back to my house for tea.

When we get in, Mum is in quite a good mood
because she has found one old persons' home which
will take a larger pet than merely a bird
or a fish.
But you may only have just the one dog,

i.e. Flossie or Ralph.

That is the catch.

Bert says he couldn't do without Flossie because
they have been each others' companions for
nearly over eleven years which, if you are a dog,
is seventy-seven.

And that is the same age as Bert himself.

He says, "We are both pensioners."

Ralph is much younger, and in dog years,
is more the same age as my dad.

If Ralph was a human being then he would
probably have been in the same class as my dad
and I expect they could have been friends.

Before supper, me, Betty Moody, Mum,
Grandad and Bert go to look round the new old
folks' home.

We all have to squish in the car.

It is called Sunset Homes which Betty and me
think sounds utterly romantic.

It is all painted the most extremely bright colours

and there is a big sticker in the entrance hall which says, 'YOU DON'T HAVE TO BE MAD TO WORK HERE, BUT IT HELPS!'

Mum says why Sunset Homes is so nice is because they have such a good sense of humour.

It's family run, which means all the people who work there are from the same entire family.

They all wear glasses.

Can you imagine my family running an old folks' home together?

Because I can't.

The lady in charge, called Pam, says the thing is, Sunset Homes understands how important it is for people to have their personal pets with them. She says she only wishes Sunset Homes could take more animals, but if they took every single person's pet it would end up more like a farm than a residence for the elderly.

Bert is quite taken with it, especially when he sees bread-and-butter pudding on the menu.

Which, for me, is my worst utter pudding.

You could probably only get me to eat it if you gave me approximately twenty-seven pounds.

Bert says the only thing he is anxious about is what will happen to Ralph the Pekinese?

He couldn't bear for him to be unhappy.

Betty says, "I'll look after him! We really love Ralph and we would really love him to be living with us on a full-time basis in our house, and I think Ralph really does like us.

I have seen him smiling, which is hard to see on a dog, but I have.

And he is always following my dad about and sometimes he just stares at him and listens to him playing on the piano.

I think he is musical, and he has probably never had a piano before, and we do, and he can listen to it whenever he likes.

He really can.

And we will bring him to visit you whenever
you like, Bert, we really will."
Bert is really pleased with this idea but Mum says
we must ask Cecil and Mol first.
And what will happen to Ralph when the
Moodys go away?
And Betty says Karl Wrenbury will look after
him because his mother is a professional dog
looker-afterer.
We phone Mol and Cecil utterly straight away
at once.
And they say, "Yes!"

It's been such an exciting day.
Almost like the kind of days Ruby Redfort has.
And now I can't wait to read about how Ruby
will escape from the evil genius, Count von
Viscount.
Because you can bet she will.

"Well, it looks like the end of the road for

you, Ruby Redfort, child defective.

Within 20 minutes, this whole room will be flooded in water. Let's see you get out of that one! I don't THINK so! Ah ha ha ha!" With that, the wicked Count turned and sealed the door shut.

It was then that Ruby remembered her little laser disguised as a decorative piece of jewellery. Ruby got to work. Within seconds she had cut through the steel handcuffs and was trying to unlock the metal door, but it just wouldn't budge. Even the tiny window was securely blocked and impossible to open. The room was fast filling with water. There seemed to be no escape ... until, in desperation, she looked up, and there, quite unexpectedly, she saw a tiny trapdoor – just big enough for an eleven-year-old girl to squeeze through.

There was just the small problem of oxygen ... breathing could be difficult ... except she did have her miniature diving apparatus, but would it give her enough time?

Finally, it is Wednesday, the big day of the school open day evening, and it is all extremely exciting and everything.
Everybody has set up their tables.

Ours is looking marvellous because we have the best exhibit.
It is a smoking volcano which actually smokes. We aren't going to turn it on until the last minute so it is more of a surprise.

Also, we don't want it to run out of smoke before the judges get to see it.

Karl has made a little helicopter
and Betty and me have made little models
of Clancy Crew and Ruby Redfort. Count
von Viscount has got them dangling over
the volcano. I made Count von Viscount. He is
papier-mâché, which is just soggy newspaper
with paste. It takes quite a lot of work to do.

The hard part is waiting for it
to dry. But it is worth it.
Karl has made a tape of the chilling
laugh – which is really in actual fact
Mrs Wilberton's but she doesn't know it.

Noah and Suzie Woo have got an actual wok in their exhibit, which is a bit like a frying-pan, but not.

It's just for show – they are not actually allowed to do any cooking in it in case it is a fire hazard. But they have made sushi, which is a fish not cooked, wrapped around a blob of rice.

And they have a display of bananas, which are not bananas but called plantain and are more like a potato pretending to be a banana.

After a little bit of looking around, everybody does their speech.

I do my speech in the style of Ruby Redfort.

Which is American.

So it sounds really good.

I say, "What I have learnt from the Ruby Redfort books is a lot."

Then I describe how we put all the clues together and one and one made two, and they all added up to mean the cup was not stolen, but just someone had been utterly forgetful, naming no names, and then blamed the wrong person. Which sometimes happens if you jump to conclusions.

And then I say, "And it is amazing what you can learn from any books you enjoy, and you don't necessarily realise you are learning something because you are so busy enjoying it."

Of course, everyone claps.

Mrs Wilberton is smiling and staring and clapping a bit too much.

And Mr Pickering says, "Nice work, girls!"

Which is a bit like at the end of the Ruby Redfort books, when Hitch always says, "Nice work, kid."

Mr Pickering says, "It's thanks to you two that we have got the cup in time for this evening. I really am very impressed with your detective work.

You could have that Ruby Redfort out of a job if she's not careful!"

Which is nice of him to say, but not true because
Ruby Redfort is not an actual real life person.
But I wish she was.
I give him one of our Ruby badges
that are home-made.
And he wears it.
It says, 'Oh boy, what a yawn!'
Anyway, everyone thinks our
speech is dreadfully
entertaining and
Call-Me-Mol says,
"Brilliant, girls!"
Karl's mother says
she is so relieved
she won't have
to discuss Karl's
bad behaviour
tonight.
And Mr
Pickering says
so is he.

And Mrs Wilberton has to say she is awfully apologetic for the mishap.
She gives Karl a box of jellybeans as a 'sorry'.

After everyone has done their speech about the learning part of their exhibit, the parents go round looking at all the models and things.

I hear Mrs Wilberton say to Robert Granger and Arnie Singh, "It's a very nicely made exhibit, Robert and Arnie, but perhaps you should stick a little more closely to the facts."
She says, "There were no chicken dinosaurs."
That is a fact.

"These bones are not 65 million years old."
That is also a fact.
I notice that Robert and Arnie do not take
any notice of Mrs Wilberton, and as soon as
the parents come around, they tell them all the
whole rubbish of how they found the dinosaur
chicken bones in Robert's garden.

Grace Grapello is sick in the toilets because she
eats most of Alexandra Holker's Victorian fudges
without asking.
They are meant to be for the visitors.
She is too ill to do her exhibit of ballet with
Cindy Fisher.
Toby Hawkling was meant to be doing the ballet
too but he got an unfortunate tummy bug in the
morning and says he is not allowed to do
anything which involves twirling
or he might faint.
It doesn't stop him eating eight egg sandwiches
though.

Cindy has to do the performance on her own.

It's not very good because Cindy Fisher has only been going to ballet for maybe two weeks and she doesn't even know the moves.

She makes most of it up.

Grace Grapello has to go home early.

Mrs Wilberton says, "It seems to me, Grace Grapello, that you got your just desserts."

Lots of people I know are at the open day evening, even Bert, Flossie and Ralph, and also my dad.

Normally Dad is too busy at the office and can't get away because Mr Thorncliff is always breathing down his neck.

Mr Thorncliff is a very strict boss and he does not like people having time off to enjoy themselves.

Dad told Miss Egglington, his secretary, who you must not call a secretary but instead a personal assistant, to tell Mr Thorncliff that he had

gone home early with a case
of
the
food
poisoning.

Which is funny because after some of Noah
and Suzie Woo's sushi he actually really does feel
a bit dodgy.

I show Dad our exhibit and Karl lights the
smoking volcano and nothing at all happens
for almost nearly one minute.

It is very thrilling.

We are on tiptoes waiting.

And then gradually there is a puff of smoke.

It looks utterly realistically like an actual volcano.

It smells a bit funny, but volcanoes do
I should think.

We will probably almost definitely win.

Then Mr Pickering comes on the loudspeaker.

He says, "Please join me in the assembly hall,
where I will be announcing the winner of this
year's book prize exhibit."

He does a little talk.

Which I forget to concentrate on halfway
through because I am watching a spider dangling

down, almost just about to land on
Mr Pickering's head.

Luckily, I come back into concentration just in
time to hear him say, "Without further ado, the
winner is…"

I close my eyes and wait to hear my name but
when I open them again the little cup is being
awarded to Alexandra Holker

because, Mr Pickering says,

"She came up with a very informative
exhibit, and to act out so much
of the Victorian age in just
a few minutes was very
ambitious."

Winner

And that, "Not everyone would be able to be Queen Victoria one minute and Charles Dickens the next."
And also, "What was left of the Victorian fudge was very good indeed."
We are utterly

disappointed

not to be the winners
and not to be awarded
the tiny cup,
and also not the mystery
prize either.
At least it was Alexandra
who won it,
who I like,
and not Grace Grapello,
who I don't.
The mystery prize turns out to be not so mysterious after all and is typical of what Mrs Wilberton would choose.

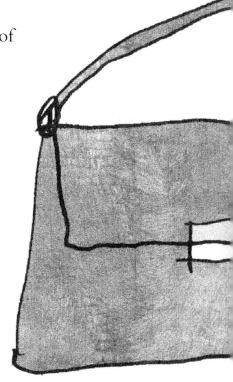

It is called *The Encyclopaedia of Ballet*, which is only a good prize if you are fascinated by ballet, which I am not. While everybody is busy watching Alexandra winning, Karl Wrenbury's smoking volcano gets caught on fire and sets the sprinklers off. Mrs Wilberton goes stark staring mad. She says her suede-look handbag is ruined.

I must say, the egg sandwiches for all the guests
are not eatable.

Luckily, the tiny sausages on sticks are fine.

When my Uncle Ted, who is a fireman, turns up
he says, "It's not really wise to have anything
smoking in a classroom.

Not without the correct level of supervision."

Mrs Wilberton is called into
Mr Pickering's office.

I think she gets a telling-off.

I hope so.

Karl Wrenbury is sent home.

And so is everybody else.

Thursday

I wake up really early, even though school has
been cancelled due to water in the classroom
causing a day off, and Mr Skippard having to
mop it all up.

He will have to wear wellingtons.

I heard Mr Skippard say to Mrs Marse,

"Mrs Wilberton can wave bye-bye to those carpet tiles in her reading corner."

Because of course they are utterly soaking wet.

And I heard Mrs Marse say, "Quite honestly, that's the least of her problems."

I am going to phone Granny and tell her about all the goings-on just as soon as I have read the last ever page in my book, RUBY REDFORT RULES.

I almost don't want to finish it,

but I utterly want to know

how it turns out.

That's the thing that sometimes happens when you read a really good book –

you just want to

read

it

all

over

again.

Ruby Redfort walked out of HQ and climbed into the waiting limousine.

What a day it had been – first rescuing her hero, Dirk Draylon, then escaping from the evil genius, Count von Viscount, foiling his dastardly plan to take over the world – as usual.

HQ were pleased with Ruby's work and told her to take the rest of the day off.

It was a shame she couldn't make it back to school in time to win the class election but hey, she had been a little tied up. Even Ruby Redfort couldn't win 'em all.

At least Vapona Begwell wouldn't be voted President. Mrs Drisco had seen to that when she caught Vapona voting for herself more than once.

Using her big toe, Ruby flicked on the super-deluxe surround sound TV.

The show was 'Crazy Cops' starring her new friend, Dirk Draylon.

It was quite something to have rescued everybody's favourite TV celebrity from certain death, and it was only a pity Ruby had forgotten to ask Dirk for an autograph.

Just then, a voice came on the car intercom; it was Hitch.

All he said was,

"Nice work, kid!"

The End

I have **utterly** just finished
the last ever sentence
when our doorbell goes.

It does a strange buzz because the battery is
needing a change.
I am really hoping it is not Mrs Stampney or
Robert Granger.
I peek
through
the
letter-box,
just in case.
I can
just
see
Ralph
the Pekinese,
so I open the door.

Luckily he is with Betty Moody.
He looks really happy.
Betty has got him a new collar.
Also, she has got my present that is from Russia.
She can't wait for me to open it.
She is hopping and so is Ralph.

You will never guess what, but it is the utterly newest Ruby Redfort edition.

Betty says it is

'hot off the press',

which

means

utterly

just

printed

probably

last

week.

It's called RUSH TO RUSSIA, RUBY!

It has a white cover and Ruby Redfort is wearing a furry hat with earflaps, and it's not even in the shops yet, and Betty got it from Patricia F Maplin Stacey herself in person, and Patricia F Maplin Stacey even wrote in it in felt-tip.

It says:

To Clarice Bean
Keep on reading Kid!
Love from
Patricia 9 Xaphin Stacey

Which is exactly the kind of thing Hitch would say.

THE RUBY REDFORT COLLECTION
by Patricia F Maplin Stacey

There was a girl called Ruby

Run for it, Ruby

Where in the World Are You, Ruby Redfort?

R U 4 Real, Ruby Redfort?

Who Will Rescue Ruby Redfort?

Ruby Redfort Saves the Day

Ruby Redfort Rules

turn over
for utterly
important information

For *Sylv*
Utterly
Thank You

An extremely special thank you to Francesca Dow, Anna Billson and Megan Larkin who were all, of course, just fabulous.

Thank you to Orchard Books for being so calm (at least outwardly) and always nice - even when I couldn't think of anything to write.

Likewise, thanks to my agent, Caroline Walsh, for the above reasons.

Thanks to my mother for being the handwriting of Patricia F Maplin Stacey.

Thank you to the Shaw Farm Video and Chocolate Tasting Society for lots of very important advice and encouraging late evening discussion.

Thank you to Rococo Chocolates whose divine chocolate bars played a valuable part in the writing of this book.

And lastly, thank you to anyone who kindly read the text for me and said they (even slightly) liked it a bit.

ISBN 1 84121 918 5

First published in Great Britain in 2002

© Lauren Child 2002

The right of Lauren Child to be
identified as the author and the
illustrator of this work has been
asserted by her in accordance
with the Copyright, Designs
and Patents Act, 1988.

A CIP catalogue record
for this book is available
from the British Library.

3 5 7 9 10 8 6 4

Printed in
Belgium

ORCHARD BOOKS 96 Leonard Street, London, EC2A 4XD

Orchard Books Australia 32/45-51 Huntley Street, Alexandria NSW 2015

ORCHARD BOOKS